CHANCES ARE

A Willow Bay Novel

by Laurie Ryan

www.laurieryanauthor.com

COPYRIGHT

DEDICATION

To Marie, for putting up with all my angst in this crazy
business. I couldn't do it without you.

CHAPTER ONE

"You may now kiss the bride."

Jackson Smith clapped, then laughed along with everyone else as his friends kissed. Josh's enthusiasm over being a married man showed big time. The man had loved Dana ever since she'd moved here and bought one of the gift shops near the beach. Josh had been waiting for this day for a long time and had even gone along with the flower-bedecked church.

What a fool. Jackson shook his head. He had nothing against women, of course. They were great as friends and offered a perspective that he found important. But once you let them into your life, everything changed and nothing lasted forever. Nope, he'd never be the one waiting at the front of the church. He'd become a born-again bachelor and nothing would change that. He was happy with his life, though an occasional dalliance wasn't out of the question. Rules were a big part of his life, but every once in a while, he liked to toss them out the window and show his appreciate for a beautiful woman.

He glanced at the wedding party again, particularly at the maid of honor. He'd seen her once before, briefly, when arresting Dana's ex-husband for forging her signature. There'd been no time to talk to her, and when he'd gone to Dana's shop the next day, she'd already left town.

Maid or matron? He couldn't see her ring finger under the bouquet she held. She intrigued him, with her long, sleek, dark hair and eyes that shone with happiness while she watched her friends exit the church. Next, she and Bernie walked down the aisle together. Josh had selected Bernadette Gibson as his best, umm, person. A nontraditional moment in an otherwise very traditional wedding.

Once again, Jackson tried to get a glimpse of the woman's left hand. Still buried under flowers, damn it. Something about her drew him in. He'd planned on ditching the reception. Weren't they all alike, anyhow? But now, maybe he'd pop in. Just to satisfy his curiosity about the mysterious woman.

As he filed out with everyone else in the church, Jackson noticed Gladys, Willow Bay's most familiar street person. "Looking mighty fine there, Miss Gladys." He took her arm as she hobbled along.

"Thank you, officer. For the compliment and the arm. I don't get around so well without my Mabel."

Jackson held back the urge to shake his head at the name Gladys picked for her grocery cart. She and Mabel were a staple in Willow Bay. She refused help with lodging but would always take food. The town had accepted responsibility for Gladys, and she probably ate better than most because of it. Still, she looked thinner today. And her white hair looked different.

"Did you get a new outfit?" Jackson asked.

"Had to have a dress for the wedding." She pirouetted with surprising dexterity. "Looks pretty good, doesn't it? Cost $3.99 at the thrift store. Even got my hair washed at Mae's."

Wondering where they'd mailed her wedding invitation, Jackson smiled at the mention of Mae's. The salon offered haircuts for free to Gladys and she loved a good deal.

"You look lovely." They'd reached her cart. "Want a lift to the reception?"

"In that thing?" She glanced at his nearby squad car. "No, thanks. Town'll think you've finally arrested me for loitering. No, Mabel and I will be just fine. It's not far. Looking forward to some good food at that reception. Oh, yes."

She and Mabel ambled their way out of the parking lot. One of Mabel's wheels wobbled, making a racket as they left. Jackson laughed. There was no one like Gladys. It hit him why she looked thinner. She usually wore two or three layers of clothing. Today, she only wore the dress, probably due to the unusually warm June day.

Yep, Gladys was definitely one of a kind.

He got in his squad car, intending to follow the procession from the church to the community hall until his phone beeped.

Damn.

A shoplifter at the hardware store. Who stole from a place like that? He toyed with the idea of calling and telling Mike he'd be a while, but if his wife was working the store alone at the moment, it wasn't fair to her. So instead of turning right, he turned left and was at the store in less than five minutes. He'd always loved the place. Full to overflowing with hardware and gift items, no tourist could resist browsing these aisles in search of treasures. And if you needed a part? It was well known that Willow Bay Hardware had at least one of everything.

Sure enough, Betty was on duty, though that wasn't necessarily better for the shoplifter. She stood behind the counter, glaring at a kid sitting on a nearby bench who was maybe all of ten years old. Way too young and in need of a good scare to set him straight, by the looks of it. Time for Jackson to put his intimidating face on. He had a special look and a low, dark tone to his voice that he used for these occasions.

"Hi, sheriff."

"This the boy?"

"Yep. Caught him stuffing candy bars into his backpack here." She plunked the offending pack on the counter and Jackson had to hide his surprise at the bounty the kid had attempted to steal.

He came around and stood in front of the slouching boy. Good. He didn't have the swagger of a habitual stealer. "Stand up."

The boy did so immediately. Another good sign.

"What's your name?"

The boy started shaking but kept his mouth tightly closed.

"Wouldn't tell me, either," Betty said.

"So you're not talking?"

The boy shook his head, even with the fear on his face.

"All right, then." Jackson turned to Betty. "He's not a local."

"I agree. I don't recognize him."

"I guess it's jail until he talks." He scowled at the boy. "Sit. Don't move."

He and Betty moved off to the side, both working hard to hide their grins.

"He's got decent clothes on and is clean, so he's probably here with vacationers," Jackson said.

"That's what I thought."

"I'll take him to the station. Sooner or later, his parents will come looking for him in a panic, though I wish I didn't have to put them through that worry."

"Maybe you'll get lucky and he'll tell you his name."

"He seems more worried about keeping that secret than what I'll do to him."

"That's because the softie in you keeps oozing out, Jackson Smith."

"I am not a softie."

"Right," Betty said, chuckling. "You don't rescue cats and dogs and take them to Bernie at the pizza joint to find homes for them, right? And you don't try to rescue the stupids who park too close to the water, either."

"That's just doing my job."

"Like I said, riiiight."

"Okay, enough. I'll take him in and wait with him."

"You'll miss the mayor and first lady's wedding reception."

The woman with the sparkle in her dark eyes flashed through Jackson's mind. He found himself wishing there was another way. "You missed the wedding."

"I'm closing up after you and the boy leave and joining Mike at the party."

"Go and enjoy. I'm fine." A momentary regret touched him. He'd never find out if the woman was married or single. Probably better that way.

They both put their stern faces back on and soon the kid was ensconced behind the screen in the squad car's back seat.

"Last chance, kid. Ready to give me your name and tell me where you're staying?"

The boy looked so little in the back seat. And miserable. He shook his head once again.

"So be it." Jackson closed the door and headed back to his two-cell station, hoping it wouldn't be long before the parents realized their son was missing. Because as much as he tried to deny it, he really did want another glimpse of the dark-haired beauty from the wedding.

~~~

Aimi Larson toyed with the edge of her champagne glass, trying to decide what had tossed her into this melancholy. Her best friend, now happily married, snuggled on the dance floor with her husband, swaying to the notes of some love song. Cheek to cheek. Heart to heart.

What did that feel like, that kind of love? She could see it in their eyes, in how often they touched. How they could be across the room and still aware of each other, how they had smiles meant only for each other. What passed between them was like a secret no one else was privy to.

Aimi had wanted that, had believed in it right up until she'd reached her testosterone limit. At first, she'd thought she wanted strength around her. Cured of that wish, she'd sworn off men, period. No one would ever make choices for her again, or keep her from getting what she wanted. So she was here solo and she'd given up on love, at least for herself. Aimi was happy for her friends, but this kind of relationship wasn't for her. She did better on her own and she liked living by herself. Being free to work long hours because she wanted to, not because she was chasing some meaningless status symbol. Free to make her own choices, not be bulldozed by some guy who thinks he knows what she needs better than she does.

Free to sleep with someone or say no. The guy at the wedding had driven that realization home. Yum. Tall, more muscular than she normally went for, but on him, it totally
~~~

worked. Short, dark hair that still showed a tight natural curl. And those eyes. Amber, like a tiger's. When he glanced her way, they'd seared right through her. She couldn't place it, but she'd seen him before.

She'd decided right then and there, standing in front of the church with her friends, that she would approach him at the reception. No strings, just a night of harmless flirting. She'd be heading back to Spokane tomorrow anyhow.

Then he'd disappeared. She'd seen him walk out of the church, then nothing. Damn it.

"Hey, why the glum face?" Dana said, sitting down beside Aimi. Her friend's curls had started to undo themselves. Dana was cursed with hair almost as straight as hers. They both fought to get curls to stay.

"Come on," Dana said. "You're supposed to be happy. Having fun."

She was right. This wasn't a moment for introspection. Her best friend had just gotten married. Aimi smiled. "I am happy. For you."

"You'll find someone one of these days, you know."

Aimi shook her head. "Not part of my agenda."

"I know you've sworn off men, but there is someone out there who's the perfect yin to your yang. I feel certain of that."

"Not for me. And I'm all right with that." Aimi buried the hint of regret. "Come on. Let's dance." She stood and grabbed Dana by the hand.

CHAPTER TWO

After dealing with frantic parents relieved to be reunited with their son, Jackson locked up the office and drove to the community hall. Knowing he should go home, that he was dancing with trouble, Jackson walked inside, oblivious of all the balloons and flowers and greenery. He didn't stop looking until he found her. On the dance floor, in the arms of Greg Michaels, the town attorney, a married man way too old for this woman. At least he could finally see she wore no ring. Without stopping to think, Jackson walked up to them and tapped Greg on the shoulder.

"Mind if I cut in?"

The surprised but pleased look on her face made Jackson smile. So she'd noticed him, too.

"Certainly," Greg said, giving her arm over to Jackson. He curled his large fingers around her soft, small, petite hand as if carrying one of his mother's prized porcelain teacups.

"I don't break easily," she said. Her voice slid over him like warmed whiskey.

"Good to know." He pulled her in tight, swaying with the slow music. Though she was a foot shorter than him, they still fit together like glove to hand. That surprised him, and pleased him in a way he didn't want to think too hard about.

They danced together in silence and Jackson lost himself in the feel of her, of them together. When she laid her head on his chest, disengaging her hand to wrap around him, his heart leaped. Attraction. That's all this was. Simple attraction. Still, having her in his arms made more sense than anything else had in a long, long while. Jackson closed his eyes and gave himself over to the music, the sensations, the way his body reacted to her. He didn't even know her name, but damn… He couldn't stop fantasizing about carrying this beautiful stranger off in his arms to some very private place.

As the music wound down, he whispered into her hair. "Want to get out of here?"

She pulled back, her eyes glazed with the same emotion he felt. Lust. Desire. A need to belong to someone, if only for a little while. She shook her head. "I'm the maid of honor."

"Things seem to be winding down."

"I can't leave until the bride and groom do."

"Looks like she's trying to get your attention."

"Oh! I'd better go. Thank you for the dance."

The woman flew away from him as if burned. At first, that offended him. He stood there, more turned on than he'd been in a long time, breathing heavily from a simple dance. And she'd run away? Or had she run away from how he made her feel? A slow smile spread over Jackson's face as he headed for the refreshment bar to cool his raging libido, keeping an eye on her as he went. They had a conversation to finish. And he was looking forward to it.

~~~

Aimi could feel his gaze on her, watching her. It should creep her out. But it didn't. The man had something. That dance had been the most sensual moment she'd ever
~~~

experienced and she wanted more. With a stranger whose name she didn't even know.

"Hold this while I check my list one more time," Dana said.

"Hmmm?"

"Aimi?"

"Yes?"

"Aimi!"

Dana's sharp voice got through the thickness clouding Aimi's brain. She turned to her friend. "Yes. I'm here. How can I help?"

"Hold this for a sec."

She took the proffered handbag. "Since when did you become a list-maker?"

"Josh. He's reforming me." Dana leaned in. "I'm doing grocery lists, logging sales activity in my spreadsheet the same day, and Duffy's on a potty and walk schedule."

"Wow. Josh has transformed you *and* your dog."

"Yes, but I make him take more time off. We got the house remodel—the one he's been working on for a couple of years—done in four months. And he's laughing more. Relaxing more."

"You two are good for each other."

"I never thought I'd find this kind of love. I'm so lucky." Dana glanced at Aimi. "Sorry."

"About what?"

"I know you want me to stop bugging you, but thinking about how good I have it makes me wish you weren't alone."

"I don't need some man in my life. I have you. I have my work. Well, I will once Greg Michaels and I finish the paperwork."

"And you had a pretty steamy dance out there just a bit ago. I could barely get your attention."

That dance. Aimi almost started swaying back and forth as she thought about it. But Dana would turn into a matchmaker with the persistence of a bulldog if she thought Aimi was interested in someone. Once her relationship with Josh had taken off, Dana had decided everyone deserved a soul mate. And she'd set her sights on finding Aimi's.

"It was just a dance." *No, it wasn't.* "And you finished everything on your list, so it's time for you and Josh to get going on that honeymoon."

The diversion worked. Dana turned her attention away from Aimi's love life.

"Six days holed up in a cabin in the hills. No internet, no phones, no tv."

"Whatever will you do?" Aimi teased. The love and excitement that filled her friend's eyes made Aimi's heart glad. "I'm so happy for you. Are you sure you want to take the dog with you?"

"You have to get back to work, and Duffy's part of our family. Josh doesn't mind."

Josh showed up to wrap his arms around Dana's waist. "I don't mind at all. But if we don't get out of here soon..."

Dana turned in her husband's arms and kissed him.

"Keep doing that and we won't make it past the cloakroom," he said.

Five minutes later, amid a shower of birdseed, they settled into their car and, with a final wave, drove off.

Aimi turned back toward the hall, so filled with happiness for her friends she almost missed him leaning against the open door. How could she miss something that fine? He wore that crooked half-smile and had his thumbs stuck in his pockets. All sexy and full of testosterone. Her body responded. Wow, did it respond. What had happened to her new rule—no testosterone in her life? Maybe, just for tonight, she should bend that rule?

He pushed off the door and closed the distance between them. Aimi's breath shortened with each step.

When he reached her, he ran his hands lightly up her arms. Aimi shivered.

"You're cold," he said, pulling his jacket off and wrapping her in it.

Since it was June and warmer than usual for the coast at this time of year, cold had nothing to do with it, but his leather coat felt so good, smelled so good, Aimi let him believe what he wanted.

He snugged the coat tighter, holding onto the edges, his eyes dipping to her lips. "I really want to kiss you."

Oh, God, did she want to kiss him. She leaned into him, unable to stop herself.

"Great wedding, wasn't it?" Bernie and Paul Gibson walked up to them and her great-smelling jacket owner stepped back, though she could sense his reluctance.

She missed him. Only a few feet separated them, but her body protested. She wanted to be nearer, needed to be close, to touch him. Everywhere.

They were talking. Bernie and Paul and this guy seemed to know each other and were talking. She should pay attention.

"—cabin is," Bernie said. "We could go give them a real shivaree."

Her sexy man, whose name she still didn't know, shook his head. "That wouldn't be wise."

"No," Bernie said. "But it would be a lot of fun."

"And it's a two-hour drive to that cabin, so four hours round trip," her husband, Paul, interjected. "Don't you think we can fill our night with better ideas, Mrs. Gibson?"

"We're going home," Bernie said, blushing as she leaned into her husband. "Looks like the hall's almost taken care of. Everyone's left and the cleaning crew will lock up."

"Okay," Aimi said. "I'll just get my things and be out of there, too."

"Have a safe flight home."

"Thanks."

They walked off and the man beside her grumbled. "I thought they'd never leave." He reached for her hand, pulling her with him as he walked to the side of the building and into the shadows, leaning her back against the wall and placing his arms on either side of her.

Trapped, and she didn't like it much.

Then he lowered his head and Aimi forgot everything except how good and thoroughly he was kissing her. His lips cherished hers, moving slowly, learning. Then quicker, deeper, harder. She clung to him, the sensations overwhelming her, a swirl of need filling her like never before. God, he knew how to kiss.

His magical lips moved lower, and she gave him more access as he slid down her neck, his hand moving up her side in concert.

More.

She reveled in his desire, in her own raging need. Her body was on fire and the only thing that would quench it was him. He cupped her breast, his thumb moving across as he sucked the skin of her neck, tearing away any reservations she might have. She needed this. Oh, God, she needed this.

He shimmied her dress off both shoulders and his sharp intake of air did more than the coolness of the night to tighten her nipples. She was outside, bare to the waist, making out with this gorgeous man. And it felt so good.

When he captured her wrists, holding them above her head with one hand, the first nudges of alarm dampened the fire within her.

Trapped.

Her breath came in ragged gasps as his lips encircled her nipple. Need and fear intermingled, confusing her, making her want to stay and run at the same time. This was too much. He was too much. She struggled, trying to pull her hands free.

He didn't let go, still ministering to her breasts. First one, then the other.

Panic rose, melding with desire. Aimi struggled again. "Stop."

"Mmmm?" he said, his mouth full.

"Stop. Please. Stop."

Finally, he pulled back. Even in the evening light, she could see the glazed-over darkness in his eyes. He was turned on. Very turned on.

"I-I can't do this."

She tugged at his hand and he let her wrists go. Only then did she draw a deep breath.

"I-I'm sorry. I-I can't."

Aimi didn't know what to say as she pulled her dress up. She couldn't explain. No words were forming, so she did the only thing her brain could focus on.

Run.

She did. Inside the building, into the ladies' room, where her purse and wrap were. She grabbed them and opened the door a slit. No one in the main room. No very handsome, very lethal-to-her-libido, man. She crept out. The community hall looked empty except for some activity in the kitchen. Racing across to the back door where her car was parked, Aimi fled the scene. Gunned her car and flew out of the parking lot, heading toward her hotel. In her rearview mirror, she saw him, standing there, staring at her disappearing car.

Aimi's hands shook on the wheel. She took deep breaths, but they didn't help. She slowed down, hoping she could make it to her hotel. Praying that he wouldn't follow her. Wishing like hell that she could have just given herself up to the moment. She thought she'd gotten past the panic. Apparently not.

Regret and mortification mingled with her diminishing fear as she pulled into her hotel and parked the car. She sat there and watched as a patrol car passed slowly by, not stopping. Then she leaned her head on the steering wheel.

She'd been so turned on. Nothing should have stopped that. She should have explained to—

Aimi sat up, realizing she'd just made out, heavily, with someone she didn't even know. He'd been there for the wedding, and Bernie had talked to him like he was a friend, so he must be a local. No, wait. She'd seen him before. But where? Hell, she didn't even know his name.

CHAPTER THREE

"Rain or shine, eh?"

"You know me so well, child," Gladys said, reaching down to pet Dana's crazy, loveable mutt, Duffy. Dana smiled as she handed the old woman a cup of coffee with her preferred *drop* of Bailey's.

Dana sat down next to Gladys with her own tea on the couch she'd installed in the store a while back. People liked to stop in and visit and half the time, they shopped as well. It was a win-win. Plus, it gave the nicest street-person Dana had ever met a comfortable place to get off her feet for a few minutes. The entire town, it seemed, had tried at one time or another to convert Gladys to indoor living, but she steadfastly chose her own way through this world and all they could do was respect that. And offer the occasional cup of coffee or dinner.

"You're antsy today," Gladys said.

"My closest friend is moving here. You might remember her from two months ago. She was the maid of honor at my wedding."

"Ah, I do. Long black hair and a joyful face, yet tinged with sadness."

What a strange way to describe Aimi. But accurate, which was even stranger. "You see people well, don't you?"

"I'm invisible, so most people show their true self around me. When's your friend arriving?"

"Anytime now. I can hardly wait."

"And she's moving here permanently?"

"Yes. Going to stay here in my back room. Things were getting a little...spooky for her in Spokane. She needed a change."

"Spooky?"

"Long story."

"Didn't I see her dancing cheek-to-cheek with our sheriff at your wedding?"

Dana laughed. "They did get rather close, didn't they? Between you and me, I thought I saw a spark there. But Aimi has never mentioned Jackson since, so maybe I was wrong."

"Hmmm," Gladys said, setting her cup of coffee on the end table. "You're a good friend, helping her like this."

"We've helped each other through a lot."

"And I'd better get out of here before the happy screaming starts. Too loud for my ears."

"You make us sound like children."

Gladys patted Dana's cheek, then stood. "You are, my dear. At least, from my perspective. Enjoy the time with your friend. I think she'll be a welcome addition to Willow Bay. A very welcome addition."

Dana and Duffy stood in the doorway and watched Gladys and her cart amble down the walk until she turned the corner. A car parked down the way and a beach-sandy family of five got out and headed into the ice cream parlor. "Come on, Duffy," she said, watching her little Borkie saunter back inside. "Aimi won't get here any faster with us standing here waiting."

Back behind the counter, Dana tried to focus on her computerized ledger, but her eyes kept drifting to the door.

Where is she?

~~~

Aimi Larson opened the glass door slowly so the bell wouldn't chime.

Ding, dong.

Oh, well, she tried. Before she could get fully into the store, she was engulfed in hugs and wild enthusiasm from both Dana and her dog.

"You're here! Finally. I thought this day would never come!"

Aimi tried to respond, but between the dog jumping on her leg and the hug-lock her best friend had on her, talking was out of the question. Her mouth emitted only garbled sounds.

"Oh, I'm sorry," Dana said, backing up. "Duffy, down!"

Aimi laughed as Duffy immediately backed off and sat. "Wow, you've got this little guy trained. Finally."

"Josh has been working with him. He's learning. Come in, come in. Wait, where's your stuff?"

"Most of my stuff is going directly to storage but my suitcases are in the car. Thought I'd say hi first."

"Smart thinking, since we mobbed you. Let me help you while the store's empty."

Together, they brought three suitcases and two boxes in from Aimi's car.

"This all you got?"

"This is all I need to live on for the moment."

They walked through a door at the back of the store into the one-room apartment that would be Aimi's home until she settled and found a place.

"It's not much," Dana said.
~~~

"It's a whole lot better than that lumpy couch in your old apartment in Spokane. And at least this time, I'll have the bed to myself. No sharing with my bestie."

They laughed as they set everything down on the bed. Aimi had stayed in this apartment before. A while back, she'd roared to the rescue when Dana's ex had tried to take half of Tangerine Treasures, the gift shop that was Dana's pride and joy.

"You saved me last time," Dana said. "Seriously. If you hadn't helped me with my ex, I don't know what I would have done."

"Glad my lawyering skills came in handy and he's out of your hair. And, in case you're interested, he's not up for parole from that jail sentence for forging your signature anytime soon."

"It's sad, though. He used to be a good guy."

"Don't you start feeling sorry for him. He raked your heart and your bank account over the coals. He's getting exactly what he deserves. *You* are way too kind-hearted."

"I know. And you're right. Enough ex talk. Let's get you settled."

Dana pointed to things as she spoke. "The sheets are clean, there's coffee for the coffee maker and your favorite creamer in the fridge, along with some munchies." She picked up a stack of towels. "These are yours."

A bell dinged.

"Ooh, a customer. You're having dinner with us tonight, okay?"

"I was hoping you'd say that. I'm starving."

"It'll be a couple hours until the shop closes, so raid the fridge. We'll pick up pizza on the way home."

After Dana went back out front to the shop, Aimi walked around the little space that would be hers for the foreseeable future. A long way from the trendy loft she'd sub-let in Spokane. But when the owners chose to return early from their year-long trip, it seemed like the perfect time for a major move, especially since life had become untenable there. It hurt, though. She'd liked some of her co-workers. It was hard to let them go.

She slumped down on the bed. Aimi was an attorney. A good one, who made good choices. Except when it came to men and jobs, apparently. Which was why she'd exorcised testosterone from her life. She was in charge. No one else. Memories of hot bodies making out against the wall of the reception building flooded her, making her want something she refused to acknowledge. Nope. She didn't need men, especially whoever that guy was. Would she run into him here? He must live nearby to have been a guest at Dana and Josh's wedding. If she did, she'd just have to make it clear to him that nothing would be happening between them.

Aimi shook her head. Pretty arrogant of her, thinking he'd even remember her. He'd probably moved on by now. Good thing, too.

She pushed him out of her mind by taking stock of her new place. Compared to where she'd lived before, there wasn't much to it. A bed, a table with a small fridge beneath it, and a hot plate and coffee pot on top. A dresser and full bathroom out the door and around the corner. Not much at all, but Dana was saving Aimi's ass. This was a new opportunity and she would rock this. Aimi unzipped her suitcase. She unpacked until her phone rang.

"Hello, Mother."

"Were you going to call and tell me you arrived in that god-forsaken village?"

Aimi rolled her eyes. "Yes, but I've only just arrived." She looked at the open suitcase on the bed. "I haven't even unpacked."

"You should have arrived an hour ago. Did something happen along the way? I knew this was a mistake. Really, you should come home. Move back in with us and ask for your old job back. That was a prestigious firm you left."

Prestigious. Yes, they certainly were that. But there was a dark side to her old law firm, one she wasn't about to discuss with her mother.

"My drive here was uneventful. Since I wasn't in a hurry, I stopped a few times along the way to take in the sights. And Willow Bay is a lovely little *town*. Really, you should come visit me."

Aimi envisioned her mother shuddering. She preferred the upper-middle-class lifestyle she and Aimi's father led in Spokane. Aimi doubted very much that she'd ever get her mother to visit Willow Bay. It wasn't her cup of tea. And Dad? Well, he'd do whatever Mother wanted him to do.

"I just don't understand why you left us to go live in such a small place."

The one time Aimi had tried to explain, her mother had excused everything almost before she'd even opened her mouth. Finally, Aimi had simplified, as she did now. "I needed a change of pace and wanted to broaden my horizons into more generalized legal issues. I explained that. And you have an active lifestyle of your own in Spokane, Mother. We only saw each other at Sunday dinner. You were busy otherwise."

"And now we won't even have that."

Had Aimi just heard a sniffle? "I'll call you every Sunday so we can catch up."

"It's not the same. You should be here, close to your parents. What if something happens to us?"

"Then I will get in the car and drive to Spokane." They'd had this conversation already.

"Well, I just don't understand it."

"I know. Listen, I have to go. I need to unpack and Dana has invited me to their house for dinner."

"I don't think that girl's a good influence on you."

"Goodbye, Mother. Tell Daddy I love him. Love you, too." Aimi rang off without giving her mother a chance to answer. She didn't like doing that, but if she didn't, she'd never get off the phone. Her mother was a tiger when she had her teeth into something and she disapproved of this move.

Maybe this wasn't a smart idea, or maybe it was. Only time would determine that. For now, Aimi set her phone down and turned to her suitcase, ready to finish unpacking and get on with this new chapter in her life.

~~~

Jackson Smith watched Gladys amble down the road, her cart leading the way. He pulled his sheriff's SUV up beside her and rolled down the window. "How are you doing today, Gladys?"

"Ah, sheriff, just the person I was hoping to see." She held onto the cruiser for support.

"Anything happening in town that concerns you?" Gladys was a regular in his office, worrying about this or that and demanding he do something about it. Just last week, she'd told him that she'd been looking at the work on the new Cannery Park to be dedicated next month.

"There aren't enough benches, Sheriff. Old people need benches," she'd said.

How was he, as sheriff, supposed to fix that? He wondered if he'd be able to help with today's concern.

"Town's nice and busy," Gladys said. "Thriving."

"So no problems?"

"Not a one."

"Then why did you want to see me?"

"I heard you're being sued."
~~~

That. He'd just gotten served yesterday. The parents of the shoplifter he'd mock-arrested the day of Josh and Dana's wedding were suing him for emotional distress. Well, not him exactly. He was named, but the primary suit was against Willow Bay for allowing him to hold a minor in custody. Like he could have gotten the boy back to them any quicker? The kid had clammed up and refused to give him a name or tell him where his parents were.

Jackson shook his head. It was an irritation he wanted to sweep under a rug. He'd been ordered to go see the attorney the city would be using. Well, not ordered, but strongly suggested.

How had Gladys found out? "Where did you hear about that?"

"I know everything that goes on in this town, Sheriff. Don't you forget it."

Jackson chuckled. The woman was right. She did have her ear to the ground. "What does my being sued have to do with you?"

He watched her forming her response. The gleam in her eyes worried him. Gladys had something up her sleeve. He wanted to question her about it but long-standing knowledge reminded him he'd only find out what she was planning when she wanted him to, and not a moment earlier.

"It has nothing to do with me. I just want to make sure you're using a local attorney. No sense driving all the way to Aberdeen when there are good people right here in Willow Bay."

Jackson had been planning to find someone in Aberdeen. Willow Bay had one attorney and Greg Michaels was past retirement age. He'd been making comments lately like he might just take that plunge.

"Isn't Michaels retiring?" Jackson asked.

"I'm sure he will at some point," Gladys said, letting go of the cruiser and grabbing hold of her cart. "But someone will take his place. So go see him. It's best for you and for Willow Bay."

She pushed off down the sidewalk. Jackson could swear he heard her chuckling as she went. Shaking his head, he wondered what that had been about. Gladys always seemed to be at the center of the action was and always had a plan. The woman was an enigma. One of these days, he would follow her and see where she went at the end of the day. She didn't act like a street person, didn't talk like a street person. And she smelled like lavender. What person with no permanent address smells like that?

A puzzle he'd have to work on one of these days. Right now, Jackson glanced at the paperwork sitting on the passenger seat. Maybe she was right. He should just go see Michaels now and get it over with. His radio squawked. A car had stalled in the middle of Willow Bay's main road.

Jackson flipped the cruiser around and headed for the call. Seeing a lawyer would have to wait until tomorrow.

CHAPTER FOUR

The next day, on his way to see Willow Bay's only attorney, Jackson slowed down, as usual, when he passed the motel. She'd stayed there. He'd followed her until she was safely home. It had been two months and he couldn't get that night, or her, out of his mind. Hell, he didn't even know her name. With a last glance, he drove to the outskirts of town and pulled up to Greg Michaels' office.

Greg had never had a receptionist, so Jackson never understood why the office had a reception area. A peel of laughter from the inner office brought an instant smile to his face. He couldn't place the laugh, but it floated on the air like a happy melody.

"Hello?" he said to the empty reception area.

"In here," Greg called from his office.

Jackson rounded the corner to see Greg at his oversized old wooden desk talking to a woman whose back faced the door. All he saw was long, straight, black hair swaying as her laughter died down.

She turned and it hit him with a solid blow to the chest. "You."

Her upturned mouth, a mouth he'd relived kissing every day and night since the wedding, drifted into an "o" of surprise as she took in his uniform. Her eyes, deep pools of dark chocolate, widened. As quickly as her expression changed, she whipped around in her chair, her ramrod straight back once again facing him. What the hell? He'd dreamed of seeing her again and she turns a cold shoulder to him?

"You two know each other from more than just that dance at the mayor's wedding?" Greg asked, looking from one to the other.

"Sort of." Jackson stifled his anger and sat down in the only chair left in the office, against a wall. He could see her cheek, though she tried to hide her face from him, leaning so her hair fell forward. Not fast enough for him to miss the deep blush, though. He relaxed in the chair. Maybe she wasn't as indifferent as he thought.

Greg continued to stare at them, waiting for a better answer. He'd wait for a long time as far as Jackson was concerned. Finally, Greg cleared his throat.

"What brings you in, Jackson?"

The woman turned toward him, just a bit, at the mention of his name.

"I need some help with a matter. I can, uh, I can come back later."

"Later won't help you. Might as well ask now, because you're going to have to deal with Aimi Larson here. I just sold her my practice."

Aimi. He liked that name. It fit her. Light and airy, like feathery kisses. Wait. What had Greg just said? "You sold your practice?"

"Yes. Just signed all the paperwork."

"I thought all that retirement noise was just that. You've been a fixture here."

"Thank you, Jackson. You know I love Willow Bay, and it's been good to me, but I'm getting old. Virginia and I would like to travel some before my days are done. So I'm retiring and we leave next week on an around-the-world cruise."

A cruise? Retiring? Jackson, usually pretty good at sorting facts out, couldn't wrap his muddled head around the man's words. "But I need an attorney. Besides, aren't you already the city's attorney?"

"Ah, that." Greg asked, then held up his hand. "Don't give me privileged information. I have already told Josh Morgan that Aimi here will be handling that." He stood up. "And I think that's my cue." He shook hands with Aimi. "Office is yours and I wish you the best of luck. Willow Bay is a great place to live."

Greg picked up a box loaded with personal items and walked past Jackson. "You're all hers now," he said, a mischievous glint in his eye. He walked out of the office with a kick to his step Jackson hadn't noticed before. Willow Bay might be losing a good attorney, but this seemed to be a good move for Greg.

When Jackson turned around, he found Aimi had moved behind the desk to Greg's chair.

"You move in quick."

Her head shot up. "I'm not a vulture, if that's what you're saying. I reached out to Mr. Michaels a while ago asking about a partnership and he came up with this idea. You just managed to get here at the changing of the guard."

"I didn't say you were a vulture."

"Your face did."

Jackson reined in his temper. He really did need an attorney. "My apologies, ma'am."

Her eyes narrowed. "So what is this about?"

Jackson hesitated. He could drive to Aberdeen. There were a couple lawyers there.

Aimi distracted him by sitting back in her chair. Even the consternation on her face didn't deter his attraction. Hiring her as his attorney was not a good idea.

"Maybe I should go to Aberdeen."

"You'd rather drive an hour or more away than have me as your attorney?" Her voice was flat, yet an undercurrent of hurt made Jackson feel like an ass. He sat down, pulled the letter from his pocket, and handed it over.

Their hands touched as she took the letter. A freaking bolt shot through him at the touch. Not good. Not good at all. Jackson almost reached out and took the letter back. Reneging wasn't in his repertoire as a rule, though, so he sat still and waited while she read it.

"Ah, so you're the one."

"Excuse me?"

"Greg told me about the case. You put a ten-year-old boy behind bars?"

"No. At least, not the behind-the-bars thing. I showed him the jail, then we sat at my desk and ate and played games until his parents found us."

"And those parents are suing Willow Bay and naming you in the suit?"

"That's what the letter says."

"I'm not sure they can do that. Law enforcement officers are mostly immune from civil lawsuits under qualified immunity."

"You're not sure? What kind of law do you normally practice?"

"Family law, mostly, though I'll be practicing general law here."

"You're a divorce attorney?" He couldn't hide his disgust. Could this get any worse? Divorce attorneys were scum-suckers who destroyed marriages for money. He'd seen that up close with his sisters. Jordan, divorced a couple years now, was still paying off her attorney. And he didn't even want to think about Julie's current predicament. Her soon-to-be-ex was taking her to the cleaners. Or, his attorney was. And now, here he sat, in front of the same type of lawyer.

"You don't like divorce attorneys?" Aimi said, watching him.

"Never seen anything good come from a divorce. Only person who seems to win is the attorney."

"I agree. Which is why I've always tried to mediate the marriages that are breaking before taking that final step."

"How?"

"I require clients to attend marriage counseling before I'll draw up papers. But you're not here to discuss my work ethic, right? You have a problem you need help with. I'm Willow Bay's attorney of record on this case. It's not a conflict of interest for me to represent you, but you need to understand that the city's interests will be first and foremost." Her steady gaze held Jackson as he wrestled with what to do.

What she'd said about divorces was completely different from Jordan and Julie's experience. They'd been, and were being, raked over the coals. And he did need an attorney, so like the smart man he was, Jackson kept his mouth shut. That didn't stop the worry from churning in his gut. He'd never been sued before. While he didn't have much, what he had was important to him. He wouldn't want to lose it to some parents with a grudge.

Aimi set the letter down and sat back. "Why don't you tell me what happened? You'd have to at some point, anyhow, as a witness for the city."

"It was the day of the wedding. You remember that day, right?" He couldn't resist the dig. He'd thought about that night so often and she seemed to have forgotten it completely. Well, maybe not completely.

She blushed, an adorable answer to his question.

"You remember." He couldn't help his smile. "Okay. Well, I was late to the reception because Betty over at the hardware store called."

Aimi sat up and grabbed a pad and pen. "Betty who?"

"Betty Johnson. She and Mike own the hardware store."

"Which hardware store?"

Jackson cocked his head. "You're not used to small towns, are you?"

"Spokane isn't Seattle or New York, but it's decent-sized."

"Well, there's only one hardware store in Willow Bay, and it's called, appropriately, Willow Bay Hardware."

She nodded, her lips thin. "Only one. Like attorney's offices."

"Yes."

"Okay. Go on."

He laid the story out. "I did not arrest the kid. Just wanted to drive home to him what shoplifting could mean. I fed him, played games with him, and didn't go to the reception until his parents showed up looking for him."

"How long was he there with you?"

"That's the crazy part. Only a couple hours."

"Doesn't seem like that's much of a reason to sue."

"I agree. Do you think we can get this dropped?"

"I plan to reach out and suggest exactly that to their attorney, see if I can get an idea how serious these people are."

"And if they are serious?" Jackson had a pretty good idea of the process, but this was important and he needed to know she could handle it.

"Making sure I know my stuff, huh? I may have been focused on family law in Spokane, but I know what I'm doing. If they are serious, then we meet, maybe in mediation, to see if we can come to a solution without going to court. If that fails, we set a court date."

Exactly what he'd expected.

"Fees?"

"I haven't had time to set up my own schedule, but the city's picking up the tab for this."

"How can they sue the city?"

"It's kind of a "failure to supervise" situation. The city didn't keep a close enough eye on you."

"That's ridiculous," Jackson said.

"Agreed, but we still have to go through the hoops."

"Good enough for me."

"Ready to move forward on this?"

"Yes," he said without hesitation. Because no matter what his brain told him, he wanted an excuse to see her again and she seemed competent. He'd try not to hold the whole divorce attorney thing against her, though the nightly calls from his teary-voiced sister made it hard.

"All right then."

"Is there paperwork we need to fill out?"

She laughed, and the lilting sound made Jackson smile again, against his better wishes.

"How about a handshake for now. I need to figure out where things are, change letterhead, etc."

Jackson stood as she came around the desk, reaching her hand out. When he took it in his, a feeling of comfort, of coming home, flowed through him. He almost flinched. He didn't do relationships. They only led to heartache. Hadn't his sisters proved that to him? Yet, when she looked up at him with those expectant dark eyes and lips that quivered between a smile and a frown, he wanted to see her again. To kiss her again.

"Deal." He shook her hand.

"Deal."

He cupped her slender hand in both of his. She felt good, fit well.

You don't do relationships, remember? And getting tangled up in a fling with someone who now lived in Willow Bay—big mistake.

Those eyes. He got lost in their deep, rich brown. She was so close. All he had to do was lean down and they'd be kissing. Kisses he'd missed ever since her disappearance.

Aimi stepped back, breaking the tender thread between them. Forgetting every reminder he'd just given himself, Jackson couldn't resist reaching for her hair, running some strands through his fingers as she stepped away. Plans be damned. He wanted to get to know her. "I never knew your name until today."

"Nor I yours. It's nice to meet you, Jackson."

"And you, Aimi. I've been thinking about you a lot." Whoa. Where had that come from?

"You're a hard man to forget." She twisted her hands together.

"I sense a 'but' coming."

"You're now my client. I don't mess around with clients."

Well, he certainly hadn't thought this through. "Damn."

~~~

Later that day, Aimi sank back into the office chair with satisfied exhaustion. She'd managed to keep Jackson Smith at arm's length, mostly, and kept things professional when she could have so easily melted into his arms. And she'd
~~~

worked hard rearranging the office to suit her needs. The desk still faced the door, which she liked. But the credenza sat against the wall behind the comfy client chairs. Aimi liked room to push her chair back, prop her feet up, and think.

She'd left the front office and supply closet as they were for now. Eventually, she'd hire help. At the moment, she needed an idea how much her client list would shrink with the change in ownership. She needed to place some ads in the local paper. Maybe pin business cards on a few bulletin boards. And notify current clients that any paperwork held in confidence by Greg Michaels would also be kept by her with the same attorney/client privilege attached.

Thankfully, she'd already designed and ordered the cards, the only thing she'd managed to do before moving. Everything had happened so fast, but after the incident at work, she hadn't wanted to stay in town for one second more than she had to. When one of the partners had assaulted her in the ladies' room, she'd run out and given her immediate notice to the only partner she respected. When he'd asked her why, she'd told him, leaving nothing out. Not that any justice would be served. To be honest, it was the last in a long string of testosterone-based events she'd come to abhor. She just wanted out. She'd settled her affairs within a week and moved to Willow Bay, only giving her new address to the moving company and one person at the office she trusted.

Panic had set in about half an hour out of Spokane, and the trip became fraught with anxiety. Pulling into Willow Bay, that had all faded.

And now here she was, with her own legal business, something she'd wanted ever since she'd headed off to law school. Grabbing her tape measure, she walked outside and was in the process of measuring the Greg Michaels Law Office sign when a car pulled up and Dana got out, along with Duffy, who raced to greet Aimi. Thank goodness she'd changed into sweats to work. She waved to Josh as he drove off, bent down and cuddled Duffy for a moment, then stood.

"I picked up some dinner for us," Dana said, carrying a bag and Duffy's bed.

Aimi looked up at the still light sky. "It can't be dinner time."

"I closed the shop half an hour ago. It's after seven. And I knew you'd lose track of time. You always were one to zone out when you had a project to complete. That's probably what makes you such a good attorney."

"I hope you're right," Aimi said. "I'm going to need that reputation to get this business off the ground."

They walked inside.

"I like how you re-arranged the office."

"It works for me."

Dana set Duffy's bed down in the corner and pointed. After turning around a few times, Duffy laid down and officially ignored them for a nap.

"His training is going well."

"Who knew you could teach an old dog new tricks?"

"Josh's self-preservation."

Dana laughed. "Most likely. Now come on. I fed Duffy before I left the store. Bernie made my favorite lasagna and I got Caesar salads to go with it." She pulled plates, napkins, utensils, and wine glasses out of her bag.

"What about Josh?"

"He ate already. He's got a council meeting. But he sent this." Dana pulled a bottle of wine out of the bag. "He'll drive us home if we drink the whole thing."

"Always thinking, that man of yours."

"Yes, he is."

They opened the wine and clinked glasses.

"To new beginnings," Dana said.

"To new beginnings. Hopefully good ones."

They dug into the food.

"Oh, my gosh, this is so good."

"It's not on Bernie's menu. She only makes it for locals who call ahead and ask for it. Even then, if she's busy, you might wait a day or so."

"I'll have to thank her for fitting one in today. I'm famished."

"You should be. You've been working hard by the looks of it."

"I even have my first client." Now, why had she mentioned that?

"Who?"

"Sorry. I shouldn't talk about it."

"Well, I bet it's Jackson. It's all over town that those vacationers are Willow Bay and he's named."

"The whole town knows?"

Dana chuckled as she swallowed a bite. "You'll have to get used to the small-town gossip mill. There aren't many secrets in Willow Bay."

"Hmmm." Did Jackson know the whole town was aware of this situation?

"Besides, I can tell by the ruddy color of your cheeks that you've seen him. Doesn't take a detective to figure that out."

"I'm not sure what you're talking about."

"I saw you two dancing at our reception. He could hardly keep his hands off you, and vice versa. You seemed completely wrapped up in each other."

Aimi wiped her mouth and took a sip of wine to cool her flaming cheeks. "We were just conversing."

"Oh, you were communicating, all right. With body language." Dana laughed, getting up to throw their paper plates in the garbage. "I've wondered why you two didn't hook up after the wedding. You'd be good together."

"There was no reason to hook up. I lived on the other side of the state."

Dana looked her friend square in the eye. "You don't anymore."

Oh, man. Aimi needed to nip this in the bud before it became the next gossip hitting the mill. She didn't need a man in her life. She didn't want one. They were nothing but trouble.

"It's unethical to sleep with clients."

"Aha! He is your client then."

Aimi ignored the comment. "So, what's this I hear about a Beer and Chowder Festival coming up?"

"Nice deflection, my friend." Dana tried to pry information out of Aimi by staring at her, but Aimi, who'd spent hours and hours in courts and at mediation tables, could duel gazes with the best of them. She stared Dana down until her friend laughed and sank back into her chair.

"All right. You win. For now. The festival isn't until the end of February and this will be our first one. We're hoping it helps with Willow Bay's winter doldrums."

"Sounds fun. I might have to try my hand at some chowder recipes."

"You?" Dana let loose a full-on laugh. "You don't cook."

"I cook. When I have time. And something tells me things move slower here. So I might actually find time to play around with some recipes."

"Well, I'll believe that when I see it." Dana's phone beeped. "That's Josh. He's done and headed this way."

Together, they tidied up from dinner, then went outside with Duffy to wait for Josh.

"You know, you should give Jackson a chance," Dana said. "He's a nice guy."

"He's a whole lot of man, Dana. More than I can deal with right now."

"I get it. But please, think about it?"

Like she could stop thinking about the behemoth who stole her breath away just by walking in the door?

Dana threw her arms around Aimi, who held on to the familiar hug like a life preserver.

"I just want you to be as happy as I am," Dana said.

"We don't all find our soul-mates as easily as you did."

"I'm not sure it was easy, but I'm glad it turned out this way. Again, for the record, if you do decide to take a run at Jackson, he's a good man."

Josh pulled up and hopped out, giving Aimi a big welcome hug. Aimi turned down his offer of a ride. After they left with Duffy, Aimi locked up and headed to her apartment, letting herself in through the back door to her home away from home. She curled up on the bed, unable to stop thinking about what Dana had said.

Take a run at him.

Jackson Smith enticed her with those amber eyes that could see right through her. Aimi traced lips that tingled at the thought of kissing him again. And when they'd touched, the power of that short physical contact had roared through her like the Spokane River.

All her adult life and half her teenage years, Aimi had wanted a strong man as her partner. Her father, God bless him, gave in to every single one of her mother's wishes, he was that smitten with her and had been since they'd first met overseas. Aimi had been granted parents who loved her with everything they had, and their marriage worked for them. Her mother ruled, and that was all right with her dad.

She'd wanted something different and had dated a few men who fit the bill, but something always felt off. Still, she'd kept on believing she wanted a dominant type right up until she ran into the testosterone wall at her former law firm. Then, when John had assaulted her—

Well, strong wasn't all it was cracked up to be, so she'd decided to give up on it. On men, to be honest.

Should she consider dating Jackson? No. Absolutely not. Most especially, she should not date a *good* man, as Dana had called him. Good meant relationships and giving over pieces of yourself until nothing remained. No relationships for her. Her life was in upheaval. She'd left everything behind, including a spacious condo, and now lived in a one-room apartment at the back of a store. She had a brand-new business, something she'd never done before, and only one client at the moment. Technically two, but for one case. She didn't have time for complications, not even a quick fling. No, it was better to keep things as they were. He's a client, she's his attorney. That's all.

Rolling over and punching her pillow, Aimi tried, unsuccessfully, to stop the amber eyes that mocked her from filling her mind.

It was going to be a long night.

CHAPTER FIVE

Jackson flipped over in bed yet again and glanced at his phone. Five a.m. He'd seen just about every hour of the night on that glowing screen. Had he slept at all?

He turned onto his back and threw an arm over his eyes. Aimi Larson, with that long, straight hair, perfectly molded body, and eyes he wanted to get lost in, invaded his thoughts. Her soft body against his hard one, her lips seeking his. He couldn't stop thinking about her, and even a cool shower in the middle of the night hadn't helped.

At least he knew her name now. Aimi. It fit her, the way she lit up when she was happy, but could slice into serious at a moment's notice.

I don't date clients.

Those words had raced through his head all frigging night. Maybe he could fire her. Cancel their handshake agreement and find another attorney out of town who would coordinate with her on the case. Except, with her just taking over the business, she probably needed clients, and she'd be royally pissed if he fired her.

Damn. He had to get her out of his mind. Throwing the covers back, Jackson sat up and checked his phone. No messages. No call-outs. Looked like it was going to be an easy start on a day when he needed to stay busy.

After he pulled on workout clothes, he locked up and drove to the gym. Which happened to be right next to the law office. He inspected the paper sign that covered the old one.

Aimi Larson, Attorney at Law.

That sign wouldn't last long in the humid seaside air.

Yeah, this had been the right way to clear the woman from his mind. Definitely. Shaking his head, he parked next door and headed inside the gym. In minutes, he was on a treadmill at a ten percent grade running five miles per hour. He pushed himself to the limit, bum knee be damned, trying like hell to forget his over-the-top attraction to Willow Bay's new attorney. After half an hour, he slowed to a walk, feeling the spent energy, his legs begging for a cool down and rest.

"Get rid of those demons yet?"

Jackson turned to see Josh Morgan walking on the treadmill next to him.

"How long have you been here?"

"Long enough to see you taking yourself to the edge. Did you find what you were looking for?"

Jackson stopped his treadmill, standing on it while he wiped his face and guzzled some water.

"I'm guessing by the scowl on your face, you didn't. Anything you want to talk about?"

"No."

Josh stared at him for a long moment. "Doesn't have anything to do with the new attorney in town, does it?"

"Nope."

"Yeah, right." Josh laughed. "You went and saw her like I asked, right?"

"Of course." Would have been nice to get a head's up that Greg Michaels wasn't the attorney, though. "How'd the council meeting go last night?" Jackson asked, trying to change the subject.

"Good," Josh answered, after a thoughtful pause. "The Beer and Chowder Festival dates are set for the last weekend in February and we've reserved the community hall."

Jackson nodded.

"And Paul's job, working with the women's shelter, is having an impact. He's been putting the kids to work on Cannery Park, cleaning up brush. They feel useful, get paid, and don't have enough time to get into trouble."

"I like that even better."

"Plus, the park is on track to be done for the grand opening in September."

"Gladys stopped me yesterday. She'd like to see more benches."

Josh shook his head, his smile wide. "Good old Gladys. Well, we can't have her worrying, can we? I think the budget can accommodate a few more."

"If you're allowing benefactor purchases of benches, I'll pay for one and dedicate it to Gladys."

"That's a great idea. I've seen that done at other parks, so I'll check into it. Oh," Josh said, reducing the speed of his treadmill. "One new thing came up. Bernie wants to increase the size of the women's shelter."

Bernie owned Square Peg Pizza Parlor and was married to Paul. Both she and her husband were forces to be reckoned with. "That's a good idea," Jackson said. "We're lucky here. We don't get too many domestic calls, but the women in this area still need a place to go and someone to help them."

"I agree. Which is why I've suggested the proceeds from tickets at the festival go to the shelter."

"Another good idea." A chill rippled through Jackson and he threw a towel around his neck. He hadn't cooled down enough and he'd pay for neglecting to warm up. "I'm going to hit the showers. Catch you later."

Josh nodded. "Hey, you should tell our town's newest attorney about the women's shelter. Maybe she'd like to get involved."

Jackson groaned and had to listen to Josh's laughter all the way to the door into the showers. Still, by the time he'd warmed up and cleaned up, he'd decided the idea had merit. He'd bet anything Aimi would like the idea. Since she was right next door, why shouldn't he stop by and tell her about it?

Stopping by had nothing to do with the overwhelming desire to see her again.

Nothing at all.

He tossed his clothes into the bag and headed out, almost whistling as he went.

~~~

Aimi got out of her car, leaned on the open door and took a deep breath. The salt air, something she'd thought she might not like on a daily basis, invigorated her. The cloud cover would disappear soon and it would be a glorious sunny day at the beach. And Willow Bay noticed when the sun was out. So did tourists. The beach would be busy today. So would shops like Dana's, and that was good news.

Maybe she'd play hooky and go for a long walk along the water this afternoon. That sounded so nice, she made a mental note to add regular beach time to her schedule. She lived in a coastal town now. Why not take advantage of it?

"Dreaming of someone?"

Aimi jumped, startled. Frowning, she turned to look at the person who stood on the other side of her car. "Jackson."

"Ah, shucks. That's awfully nice, you dreaming of me."

Heat filled Aimi's face. "That's not what I meant."

"That's what I heard."
~~~

"Well, it wasn't...oh, never mind." Aimi slammed the car door shut and rummaged in her bag for her office keys, almost dropping the supplies she'd brought.

Jackson took the extra bags and waited, close behind her, while she opened the door. Too close. His proximity added to the panic building inside her. Cloying panic.

"Back off," she said, hearing the breathiness of her voice. She pushed the door open and hurried inside.

With a frown marring that gorgeous face of his, Jackson followed more slowly. He set the bags down and looked at her. Several feet separated them, but she couldn't shake the closed-in feeling that threatened to overwhelm her. When he took a step toward her, she held out a hand to stop him.

Thankfully, he froze. "I'm sorry. I didn't mean to upset you."

"You...you didn't."

"Yes, I did."

Aimi shrugged. "I don't like people getting so close to me." *That night, outside the wedding hall, the heat between them, the closeness...*

"At least, not without permission," she added.

Aimi rolled her shoulders to slough off the anxiety. It helped. Sort of. Just having the tall, dark, and handsome sheriff here made the office seem small.

"Someone hurt you." His voice went granite hard.

Since this was a discussion Aimi didn't intend to have with him, she raised her chin. "No."

He eyed her for a long moment. Aimi held his gaze, refusing to be the first to look away.

"There's a story inside you, Aimi Larson, and I intend to find out what it is."

If anyone could, Jackson could. That voice of his, once he dropped the hard edge, could melt icecaps.

"You're my client."

"Yes. You've mentioned that before."

"And we don't know each other well enough for revelations."

"But we will."

Aimi's eyes widened.

Jackson pushed off the desk, keeping his distance. "I came by to tell you that Bernie over at Square Peg is putting together a coalition to enlarge our women's shelter. I thought you might be interested in being part of the process."

He still watched her, those eyes seeing everything. Aimi steeled herself not to react. "I would. I'll have to stop by and see her."

"Great." Jackson smiled, that megawatt grin that turned her legs into jelly every time. "Then I'll see you later."

"Later?" She croaked the word out.

"Yes. As you're fond of reminding me, I'm your client. Besides, I'm bound to see you somewhere. Small town and all. Bye for now." Jackson winked at her and was out the door before she could answer. Aimi slumped down in the receptionist's chair. All the goodness of that fresh sea air had dissipated. Why did she let Jackson get to her so easily? The man could tear down her defenses with a smile. She had to constantly shore them up. She didn't need a man in her life. Didn't want a man in her life. Men controlled and she was never going to be under a man's thumb again.

Having sufficiently stiffened her backbone, Aimi decided to put Jackson out of her mind. She picked up her bags and went into her office. Right there, front and center on her desk, was the folder about the suit against the city and its sheriff. No matter how much the flash of his golden-brown eyes disarmed her, she could not be attracted to Jackson Smith. She absolutely could not. Still, the memory of that kiss, so good, so deep, her back against the community center wall, her hands learning the muscles of his back as his covered her breast. Aimi shivered. She couldn't forget that night. Lord knows, she'd tried. Would it be so hard to scratch an itch with him?

Yes. Itches could lead to more and he was the sheriff. Used to control. Not the kind of guy she wanted to be with if she ever chose to date again.

If she didn't see him, she wouldn't think about him, right? Nodding her head, Aimi opened his folder. Time to make those calls and get this frivolous case ended. The sooner, the better.

CHAPTER SIX

Jackson drove his cruiser down the sandy road and turned onto the beach. Washington State Police patrolled this stretch as it was considered a state highway, but he liked to make his presence known as well. The abundant sunshine had drawn out the summer crowds, that was for sure. Everything looked peaceful. Kids, parents, and dogs all playing in the surf. Kites flew in the ever-present ocean breeze. Rolling down his window, he enjoyed the sound of waves pounding their way to shore. The tide, almost slack, had gone out further than usual and he stopped to remind several cars parked too close to the water that within a couple hours, the water would reach them and they'd be stuck.

A group on horseback headed back to their trailer and the gulls flew overhead, searching for food the tourists loved to throw to them.

Another peaceful summer day in Willow Bay. He loved the town like this.

A scream near the water got his attention. Not a fun scream, but one filled with panic. Jackson zeroed in on a woman standing in knee-deep water, waving her arms. He slammed the cruiser into park and leaped out with the float he kept in the passenger seat. He raced toward her.

"Please," she cried. "My son's out there." She gulped air. "He wanted to swim. I told him no. I only turned my back for a minute and he was gone!"

Jackson scanned the water. There. Something bobbed out there. Too far for someone without strong swim skills. Riptides were dangerous around here. A group had formed around them and Jackson barked out orders as he pulled shoes off, peeled out of his socks and shirt, and emptied the pockets of his shorts.

"Call 911. Tell them we need the Coast Guard and an ambulance."

He didn't wait for an answer. He threw the float string over his shoulder, sped into the water, and dove over a wave. Always a strong swimmer, Jackson took a bead on what he'd seen and swam with sure, strong strokes through wave after wave. Before long, he felt the riptide grabbing him. The boy had definitely gotten caught in it.

Closer now, he took precious moments to reset his direction. It was definitely the kid, and he was struggling. Good, that meant he was still alive. It took another minute or two of powerful strokes for Jackson to reach him just as the boy's head disappeared underwater. He grabbed for him.

"Gotcha." Treading water, Jackson felt for a pulse and found a thready one. But no breathing. Probably swallowed water. He pulled the boy into his chest, wrapped his arms around him, kicking to stay afloat, and performed a modified Heimlich maneuver. It took two tries before the boy coughed, spitting out water. He coughed some more, then began to struggle in Jackson's arms.

"I've got you," he said to the boy. "Stop fighting. I can get you back to shore if you work with me."

After repeating himself a couple more times, all the while keeping a tight hold on the boy pummeling him, the boy sagged in his arms, passed out. He had a pulse and was breathing, so Jackson put him in a rescue hold and turned toward land. They'd floated a lot further out than he'd hoped and it was going to take everything he had to get back. He'd barely started when he heard the whine of a Coast Guard zodiac.

They reached him in seconds and hauled the boy, then him, out of the water.

"Thank God you got here. I wasn't sure I could make it back to the beach."

The man handed him a towel. "You'd have made it."

They reached the beach quickly. Jackson stepped out of the Zodiac and took the boy, maybe ten years old, in his arms. The boy clung to him, but he'd stopped crying. Jackson had barely made it out of the ankle-deep water before the mother was on him, pulling the boy, who'd renewed his sobbing, from his arms.

"He's all right," Jackson said. "I see the paramedics coming now. They'll want to check him out, but he seems to have come through this just fine."

"Thank you. Thank you so much. You saved my son."

"All in a day's work, ma'am."

After the boy had been taken away in the ambulance, the mother following in her car, the crowd started to disperse. Jackson looked around for his clothes and found Aimi standing beside his patrol car clutching a neatly folded shirt.

He walked toward her, exhaustion dragging at him. He was getting too old for these kinds of rescues. They needed a stronger presence on the beach, but every time he approached the council about it, he ran into the hard wall of this being the state patrol's domain. Still, he'd have to try again.

"Hey," he said to Aimi. She looked good. Windblown, strong, her eyes bright.

"Hey, yourself," she answered, handing him his shirt. "That was pretty amazing, what you did."

Jackson pulled the shirt on, but not before noticing her downward glance. She seemed to like what she saw.

"All in a day's work."

"Really? You do that regularly?"

He rotated his arm, easing a growing stiffness in his shoulder. "Not every day, thank goodness. But it happens too often for my comfort."

"There are signs everywhere warning about the tides."

"Not everyone listens. This mother did. She warned her son. He didn't listen."

"Ah, he's at that bullet-proof age."

"Apparently," Jackson said, leaving the items from his pockets lay for now. His shorts would dry quickly, but he'd feel salty and sandy until he could get a good shower. He sat on the tailgate and pulled on his socks and shoes, wiping as much sand off his feet as he could.

"Well, that was about the scariest thing I've ever seen," Aimi said.

"It was nothing. Really."

She moved close enough that he could smell her perfume. Jasmine, or something like it. Floral and spicy. She put her hand on his shoulder. "No. It wasn't nothing. You saved that boy's life. That's something pretty special."

They were almost eye to eye. So close, Jackson could see flecks of gold in her dark eyes. Her lashes dipped, then rose, but what drew him most were her lips. So perfectly kissable. God, he wanted to. He wanted her in a way that scared the hell out of him. He didn't do relationships. He sure as hell didn't do marriage.

He reached up, brushed a windblown lock off her face, and tucked it behind her ear. Her eyes were wide, but she didn't flinch. That was progress from this morning.

"I'd really like to kiss you," he whispered.

He didn't reach up and pull her to him. He waited until she leaned forward ever so slowly. She paused, so close he could feel her breath.

"This isn't a good idea."

He tugged her the rest of the way until their lips met and the sensations exploded inside him. He shifted to pull her in tighter and she moved with him, her hands cupping his face as he tightened his hold on her buttocks. Everything faded except her. Here. Now.

"Ahem," a voice said behind them.

Aimi lurched back, her face flaming as they noticed Josh, in running gear, standing there grinning. Jackson had a pretty wide grin on his own face, which didn't help his cause with Aimi. He could damn near see the curtain-of-no-emotion slide down her face. Damn. That must serve her well in court.

"So, you two an item?"

"No," Aimi said.

"Yes."

"What?" She stared at Jackson. "We are *not* an item."

"People on the beach say differently," Josh said, waving his hand around at the few people watching them. Aimi's curtain slipped a bit as she put a hand to her cheek.

"Gotta go finish my run. Nice job today, Jackson." He laughed again and headed out.

"He meant about you saving that boy's life, right?"

Jackson shrugged, unable to stop the pleasure flowing through him. His body was awake and he felt better than he had in a long, long time. "Maybe."

Aimi put her hands on her hips. "He better have been talking about the boy. Because we— " she pointed between them, "are not an item. You're my client."

"If that's all that's standing in our way, then you're fired."

Shock ripped that curtain off Aimi's face. "W-what?"

"You heard me."

"You can't fire me."

"Can too."

She straightened into her legal backbone. "No, you can't."

He crossed his arms over his chest, thoroughly enjoying this. "What legal precedent says I can't?"

"Well...none, but, well..."

"You said well twice."

Her eyes flashed fire. "I know. Look, there aren't any other attorneys in Willow Bay."

"I don't mind a drive."

"You won't find an attorney as good or as doggedly stubborn as me. I will fight for you all the way."

Stubborn. That was a fact. "That may be true."

"So don't fire me."

"Then don't draw that imaginary line so tight."

"I could be disbarred for fooling around with a client."

"Really?" He hadn't thought about that.

"Yes." She used her hands for emphasis.

"Hmmm. I hadn't thought about that." Jackson reached for her hand and tugged her gently until she stood between his legs. "I guess, then, we'll just have to be careful about who sees us."

She didn't resist. At least, not much. That emboldened him. Jackson ran his hands up and down her arms.

"I'm trying to be serious here," she said, her voice just a whisper. "I need you as a client. I need a good reputation to get more clients. And, I don't need— "

"What?" He began massaging her neck and Aimi closed her eyes. "What don't you need?"

"I really don't need some man overpowering my every decision." Her eyes flew open. She hadn't meant to say that. "I'm sorry," she said. "I-I can't do this." She backed up, the apology written on her face, then raced off down the beach.

Jackson sat there for a while, watching her swinging ponytail fade into the distance, then turning to watch the waves roll into the shore. Something... No. Someone had scared her, made her wary. His hands clenched into fists. He'd find out who and deal with it because Aimi deserved nothing but happiness in her life. Selfishly, he wanted to hear her laughter, let it swirl around him and remind him how much light and beauty there was in the world.

He stood and closed the cruiser tailgate, thinking about his sisters. What would he do if someone scared them? His hands gripped the tailgate, hard. He'd contemplate murder, that's what he'd do. He'd seen them through school and walked both of them down the aisle. Back in those days, he'd thought maybe he'd find his own true love. That was before they'd each cried on his shoulder during their completed and pending divorces. Jackson had decided then and there that marriage wasn't for him. Not if it meant that kind of heartache.

Though Aimi, with her expressive eyes, heady scent, and that I-want-you-but-won't-go-there attitude mellowed those feelings. Yep. He was in trouble. Aimi was what he wanted. Now all he needed to do was figure out how to wrap his head around it. And how to convince her to give them a chance.

~~~

Walking into Square Peg Pizza, Aimi was still off-kilter from her conversation with Jackson. She couldn't be with him. Didn't want to be attracted to him, had so many reasons not to. More reasons than there were to give in. Except, when he held her, kissed her, she forgot everything except the sensations evoked by his touch. Love, family, home.

No.

No. No. No. She was not going to do this.

"Can I help you?"

Aimi refocused on the redhead behind the counter. "Hi, Bernie."

"I know you. Wait, you're Aimi, Dana's friend, right?"

"Yes. I've moved here now. In fact, I bought Greg Michaels' practice."

"He's been talking about retiring for a couple years. I'm glad to hear he finally did it. Welcome to Willow Bay."

"Thanks. I was, um, talking to Jackson Smith, and he mentioned you've got a crew working on expanding the women's shelter."

"I am. We hit capacity way too often, so it needs to be bigger. I just met with a few people to go over what we need and how we can make it happen."

"I'd love to be involved, if that's possible."

"The more the merrier. We planned to do some brainstorming and come back together in a couple weeks." She pulled out her phone. "What's your phone number? I'll notify you when we get that set up."

They exchanged cell numbers, then Bernie plopped down on a stool. "Man, I just do not have the energy I used to. And if I don't stop having to pee every time I stand up, I'm never going to make it." She rubbed her stomach.

"Are you pregnant?"

Bernie nodded.
~~~

"Congratulations. When are you due?"

"Not until early March. Not sure how I'm going to wait that long to hold this little bean."

Aimi smiled, feeling a pang of longing that surprised her. She'd never thought about kids. Had never been around them enough to even know if she liked them. "You look great."

"That's what Paul keeps trying to tell me, too. Not sure I believe him."

"Well, you do."

"Thank you. You know, if you're looking for ways to be involved and get the word out that you're the new lawyer in town, think about getting involved with the Beer and Chowder Festival."

"Dana told me about that. Good idea."

"Just let Josh know you want to be part of the process and he'll get you involved. But be warned. He's very good at delegating, especially since he has a hot wife to get home to."

Aimi laughed.

"So," Bernie said, "if you don't mind my asking, are you seeing anyone?"

Just one super-hot sheriff. Except he wasn't in her life and she wouldn't let that happen. Still, she looked away, trying to hide the blush heating her cheeks. "Nope."

"Look," Bernie said, watching her closely. "I'm not the most diplomatic person around, so I'm just going to come out and ask, because we take care of our own around here. Do you have first-hand experience with women's shelters?"

Aimi took her time answering. She wanted to make a home here and didn't want to alienate anyone, but discussing her life wasn't generally something she did. She'd always thought her life worked better if she kept things close, but had it? Aimi had moved here to make a fresh start. Maybe she should try opening up. Just a little.

"I haven't spent time in a women's shelter, but there have been issues. Because of them, I cut all ties with my life in Spokane, except for family, when I moved here."

"I lived on the street. Willow Bay turned me around and saved my life. So we all have pasts." Bernie reached over and patted Aimi's hand. "And we all deserve bright futures."

A serious mist filled Aimi's eyes. She never cried, so she sniffed to hold back the unusual tears. "Thank you."

"I know you've got Dana, but if you ever need anything. An ear, a hand with a sledgehammer in it, you call."

After saying goodbye, Aimi drove back to the office thinking about her conversation with Bernie. Already, the friendships she was forming seemed potentially deeper than her relationships in Spokane, except for Dana, of course. A lot of positivity swirled around this move she'd made. Aimi smiled, feeling really good about things for the first time in a while.

Her phone rang as she parked her car.

"Have you come to your senses yet?"

Always straight to the point, her mother. And since when was the beach godforsaken, as her mother loved to describe Willow Bay? "Hello, mother. My senses are perfectly intact."

"I can't always know you're safe when you're so far away, Aimi. You are my life."

Aimi knew just how true that was. Her mother lived vicariously through her only child. She also worked very hard to design that child's life in the way she saw fit.

"I'm fine, mother. Settling in well. Dana's been a huge help."

"That girl's the reason you moved."

"Part of it. It's good to be close to her again."

"I don't think she's a good influence on you. You should come home."

And not work, and look for a husband to care for her, and run a traditional household like her mother. This mantra was on constant repeat in Aimi's brain thanks to all the reminders and innuendos her mother sent her way. "How's Daddy?"

"Your father is as he always is. Now, did you really start a practice there? Do you know how much time your own business will take? You'll never have time to meet a nice man, get married, and give me grandbabies."

Jackson popped into Aimi's mind, including the very tempting idea of doing the necessary to have babies. She steadfastly clamped the lid on that box and shoved it to the recesses of her mind. "Mother, we've had this conversation. I'm not interested in babies, at least not for a long while. I want a career, a life. I'm not ready to settle down and I don't know when, if ever, I will be."

Silence answered her. Growing up, all their arguments had ended in her mother's disapproving silence. Aimi could still feel the guilt stretching and growing. Invariably, she would give in to her mother's wishes because she couldn't stand the weight of the quiet.

Stealing her resolve, Aimi threw out an olive branch. "You and Daddy should come visit me, see my office and how my life is here. I think you'd like it." At least, her father would, though he wouldn't say he did unless Aimi's mother gave it the nod.

When her mother didn't answer, Aimi gave up. "I need to get to work, mother. You can continue the silent treatment if you wish, but know that I love you and I'm happy here. I hope you come to terms with that."

She hung up the phone because there was nothing more to be said. Aimi really did love her mother, and she respected that she stuck to her opinions. But Aimi couldn't—no, she wouldn't—live according to her parents' expectations. Her life was hers to design. Not her parents', not some guy's. Nobody's but hers.

Jackson wanted to design her life, too, at least part of it. That kiss on the beach, in front of the whole world, still made Aimi's blood sing. The man could kiss. He made her feel things she'd purposely suppressed and damn it, she wasn't ready to open that box again. He was pushing her, and she didn't like it.

Liar.

Aimi let herself into the office, still unsure what to do about the sheriff. Her body said go for it, but her heart, logical for the first time in, well, ever, reminded her that pushy men had only made her life miserable.

And there sat Jackson's file, in the middle of her desk. Damn. She'd forgotten to tell Josh and Jackson about the phone call that morning. She'd have to contact them.

But not right now. She needed distance. Mental distance.

Settling in to work on some marketing, Aimi pulled up Greg Michaels' client list on her computer. Twenty minutes later, she was still staring at the screen with nothing done.

It's too quiet in here. She grabbed her phone, blue-toothed it to the speaker, and pulled up her workout playlist. Soon, music was blaring through the office. Aimi chair-danced in time to it, trying to drive out thoughts of Jackson so she could get some work done.

Not an easy thing to do.

CHAPTER SEVEN

The sun, well risen, beat down on Jackson as he ran. He'd been out for an hour, testing his leg as he regularly did, racing against the ever-present breeze. The doctors had told him the knee was as good as it was going to get. Truth be told, he was the only one who noticed the slight limp. He should thank the football injury. It had changed the course of his life, and he loved being a sheriff. Especially in Willow Bay.

Blowing out a breath as he gave into the day's heat and slowed down, Jackson walked back along the beach for a mile or so, cooling down and enjoying the summer rumble of the ocean. Deep breaths of cleansing sea air relaxed him even further.

When his phone rang, he answered it automatically, hoping it wasn't a sheriff's matter on his day off. Getting time off the clock was rare for him. More often than not, he got called in anyway.

"Hello?"

All he heard was sobbing. Alarmed, Jackson yanked the phone back to see the caller's name.

"Julie? Julie, is that you?" He'd just spoken to his sister last night and everything had seemed all right. Well, as all right as going through a nasty divorce could be.

The sobbing increased.

"Julie, if you don't calm down and talk to me, I'm calling 911 to have them do a welfare check on you."

"No. Don't. Call."

Then calm the fuck down. Jackson sank to the sand, gripping his phone tight. "What's wrong, Sis?"

"Everything!" The sobbing went up a decibel.

"Are you all right?"

"N-no."

"That's it. I'm calling 911."

"No. Don't. Please." He waited as the sobs grew further and further apart and her staccato breaths calmed down.

"I'm s-sorry," Julie said. "I just didn't know who to call, and I need a shoulder to cry on."

"Honey, you can always cry on my shoulder. You just can't scare the hell out of me like that ever again. You're really okay?"

Another staccato breath. "I'm better. Just hearing your voice helps."

"Good." Jackson loosened his grip on the phone and stared out at the ocean, calming his own breathing. "Now, tell me what's got you so upset."

Julie hiccupped. "He wants… Oh, God, I can't even say it."

"What?" Jackson loved his sisters, but sometimes they drove him nuts. "What does he want? Your camera?" Julie was an accomplished photographer and that's all he could think of that would affect her this way.

"No! He wants Garvey!" She started sobbing all over again.

Garvey? Her cat that no one can get near without getting scratched? "He wants the cat?"

"Yes," she said, crying. "He says Garvey is more his than mine, so he should get custody. I can't live without Garvey, Jackson. I just can't."

All this drama over that cat? His sister was normally more level-headed than this. There had to be something else going on. "What else does he want, Juliebud? What aren't you telling me?"

Julie sniffled. "He's trying to clean me out. The cat, the house, the business. He wants everything."

"The house? But that's the home we grew up in. He can't make you sell that."

"His attorney says he can." More sniffles. "Says we have to split everything right down the middle and he wants his fifty percent. I-I don't have the money to buy him out, Jackson. I'm worried I'll have to sell the house."

When Julie got married, Jackson and their sister, Jordan, had gifted her the house they'd all grown up in and transferred it into her name. In retrospect, that might not have been such a good idea, but neither Julie nor her ex made a lot of money at their dog grooming business, so it had seemed right at the time.

"Well, if it comes to that, we'll come up with the money somehow," he said. "What does your attorney say?"

"He's worthless. Said Scott's attorney is following the letter of the law."

Divorce attorneys. Bah! They were like the worst type of riptide, stealing until nothing is left but a few grains of sand. Jackson looked out over the water which, at the moment, didn't do much to quiet the broken, sharp-edged marbles rumbling around in his stomach. Glancing each way, he tried to think this through. When he saw a familiar face, he realized he needed a second opinion.

"Hey, Juliebud, I've got an idea, but you need to give me a little time. Let me call you back, okay?"

"Sure. Just don't take too long. We go to mediation in a couple weeks."

"You're not going anywhere without me at your side. Sit tight. I'll get back to you."

Jackson stood and stuck his phone in the pocket of his shorts to head toward the surf. And Aimi Larson. He needed advice. Also, if he was being honest with himself, this was the perfect excuse to see her again. Today, she wore jean shorts with rips in strategic places and a white tank top that showed off the bit of tan she'd gotten since moving here. Her dark hair hung in a ponytail through a hole in her bright yellow sunhat.

When she turned and saw him, Jackson took a memory picture of the perfection in front of him. Aimi, with a smile meant only for him, stood in ankle-deep water with the sun-sparkled water rolling in behind her. A few fluffy clouds dotted the sky, an ideal beach scene.

"Hey, Aimi," he said, taking a big gulp of air to remind him he was still in his body, not having some ethereal experience.

~~~

Men weren't allowed to look as hot as Jackson Smith, were they? In cargo shorts and carrying his t-shirt, he rivaled any romance cover she'd ever drooled over. His muscles moved in all the right ways as he walked toward her with that lopsided smile on his face.

She smiled as well. Hard not to when Jackson was her view. Wow. The man was built. He did things to her. Made her want to do things with him. She couldn't help it.

Damp hair meant he'd been running. Or swimming? No, he probably only did that in rescue situations.

"Hey," she said back to him. "Been jogging?"
~~~

He nodded, then slipped off his shoes and socks and joined her in the ankle-deep water. "You out for a walk?"

"Yes. I wanted to get in some sunshine before it disappeared. I hear clouds are rolling in for a couple days starting tomorrow."

Jackson nodded. "Mind if I walk with you?"

"Not at all." Something hovered at the edge of her mind, something she needed to tell him, but all she could think about was her urge to walk him straight into her bed. So much for her plan not to let this man in her life. Luckily, Tangerine Treasures was still open. No way she could pop in for an afternoon tryst.

"Do you own your own place here?" she asked, then chided herself. He might think she had nefarious intentions. She'd better get herself under control or she'd attack him right there on the beach.

"I just bought a house. It's my first place, though, so a little short on furnishings at the moment."

"Congratulations on becoming a homeowner."

"I suppose it was about time."

"Do you live alone?" Aimi had no idea where that question had come from. She kicked at the surf.

Jackson eyed her for a long moment. "No roomies, no girlfriends. No wives. Not even a pet. Just me."

Aimi's heart swelled at the response. She didn't want to think about why she felt so happy at the moment. When Jackson reached for her hand, she turned to look at the ocean, aware that she was grinning like a teenager. Lordy.

When she turned back toward him, he reached for her ponytail and gave it a gentle tug. "You do strange things to me, Aimi Larson."

"Likewise," she whispered back.

"I'm not big on relationships."

"Too many go sour?"

Jackson glanced out at the ocean for a moment. "Something like that."

"Oh." Aimi tried to hide her disappointment. Really, this was better. She didn't want a man in her life. Didn't need a man, and certainly didn't need to be controlled or told what to do or not do. She pulled her hand and ponytail free and stepped back.

He frowned but didn't stop her. "I pretty much raised my sisters."

Aimi struggled to wrap her head around the change of subject. "What happened to your parents?"

"Killed in an accident when I was eighteen. My sisters were just hitting their teens."

"I'm so sorry," Aimi said, taking a step closer.

They started walking again, heading back toward town.

"It was rough at first, but we made it through. They graduated from college debt-free, which makes me pretty proud. Then they both got married. And divorced."

That explained why Jackson didn't like divorce attorneys. "That must have been hard on you."

"It was. Is. My sister Julie's divorce isn't finalized. In fact, I just got off the phone with her and she's pretty upset. Scott, her ex, left her for another woman and now he wants half of everything, which includes our family home. And he wants the cat, which for some reason has Julie more upset than anything."

"In my experience, the pet is an emotional ploy to get someone to cave and give away what the person really wants. Usually money."

"Yeah."

"What's her attorney saying?"

"That the law is on the ex's side when it comes to dividing finances."

"That's bullshit," Aimi said, waving her hands in the air, warding off the negativity.

"That's what I thought."

Aimi hated that Jackson's sister had to go through this. And that Jackson was upset. She wanted to smooth the deep creases in his forehead.

"Where does your sister live?"

"Seattle."

So, Washington State, which was good, since Aimi was licensed here. "I could talk to her if you'd like."

"I wanted to ask but didn't know how. I'll pay you for any time," Jackson said.

"First things first. I'm not going to take over from another attorney without a pretty darn good reason. But maybe I can offer some advice."

"Anything would be helpful. I'm really out of my league here."

"And this is my wheelhouse."

"I'm trying really hard not to hold that against you," Jackson said.

Normally, that would have irritated the hell out of Aimi, but when he put his arm around her shoulder, she forgot, well, everything, except the feel of walking close beside him. Though he was easily a foot taller than her, somehow their steps coordinated well. The heat rolling off his body enveloped her in a haze that didn't feel at all bad. In fact, it led her back to her first thoughts when she'd seen him today. Where was the nearest bed?

Maybe if she had a romp with Jackson, she could push him out of her mind. Scratch that itch and get on with the things she should be doing. Except, they lived in the same town. A very small town with very big eyes and ears. And what if she fell for him, a very real possibility? So many things could complicate this. Aimi didn't have one single idea how to handle any of it. Him. How to apply limits. No holding on. No emotions.

As they walked off the beach to Dana's shop and Jackson pulled his t-shirt on, Aimi watched him. The happy satisfaction on his face made her heart swell. The guy did something to her, touched her in a way she'd never felt before.

Which meant no emotions wasn't an option.

When they reached Tangerine Treasures, Jackson gave Aimi his sister's phone number. "Thank you again for being willing to talk to her. I'll call her now and let her know."

"I'm happy to, Jackson."

He smiled at her and leaned down as if he was going to kiss her. Right in front of the windows of Dana's store. Aimi, eyes wide, stepped back, remembering her embarrassment on the beach. One public kiss was enough.

Jackson glanced around and chuckled, then leaned forward to kiss her on the cheek.

"I'll talk to you later, then," he said. Plunging his hands into the pockets of shorts already threatening to slip, he turned and walked away.

Aimi stood there, hand on her cheek, watching the man she couldn't stop thinking about walk down the street. And knowing the truth.

She was in deep trouble. Very, very deep.

CHAPTER EIGHT

As Jackson walked up to Josh and Dana's place the next night, he stopped to admire the impressive house. One of several old mansions located in this part of town, Jackson had been sad to see it fall into disrepair. Then Josh bought it and brought it back to life, albeit slowly, until Dana required the renovations be done quickly once they'd decided to marry. Jackson was excited to see the inside, though the dinner invite had come as a surprise.

The door opened before he could knock.

"You going to stand out there all evening?" Josh said.

"Just admiring the old girl." Jackson stroked one of the columns holding the porch roof up. "She looks good."

"And I've got the blisters to prove it." Josh laughed as he ushered Jackson into the foyer.

"You still working on it?"

"Finishing touches only, mostly on the third floor, my home office."

"So let me get this straight. You've got your mayor's office, your accounting firm office, and now a third one here at home?"

"Hey, I do a lot of desk work. Besides, the mayoral one is temporary."

It was Jackson's turn to laugh. "That's what you think."

"Are you men going to stand in the hall all night or join us?"

"Us?" Jackson looked at Josh, who shrugged and left him to follow along to the living room. Sitting next to Josh's wife on the couch, looking embarrassed while she glared at a smug Dana, sat the very lovely Aimi Larson.

Jackson grinned. This evening was looking up. "What a nice surprise."

Dana stood to give Jackson a friendly hug. "Aimi stopped by to drop something off and I invited her to stay."

And probably didn't tell her I was coming.

"Perfect," Jackson said, his grin widening.

"Can I get you a beer or something?" Josh asked.

"Coffee for me. I'm the only coverage this weekend."

"Coffee it is. Black, right?"

"I'll help you," Dana said, hurrying after her husband.

"Yes, thanks." Jackson sat down next to Aimi, throwing his hand over the back of the couch.

"Did you go back to your office after you visited Dana yesterday?"

Sitting so close made him want to run his hands along her soft skin.

"Yes, I did. And I spoke to your sister."

He nodded. Julie had called him to thank him, in a much calmer state than during her previous call. "Julie said she'd talked to you."

"She's getting railroaded. I gave her some ideas and suggestions to bring up with her attorney. She seemed to like most of them. She's going to call me back and let me know how it goes. She may switch to my services based on that, but I told her she'd have to be clear with him why she was changing."

"She mostly needs to know someone's on her side," Jackson said. "This has been really hard on her."

"Divorces are never easy, and it does seem like that ex of hers is trying to fight for things he has no right to get."

"Like the cat?"

Aimi laughed. "Actually, he has more right to the cat than she does. He found her, he brought her into the relationship. Though I hope he doesn't push the issue. Sounds like Julie and Garvey really hit it off."

"That cat adores Julie. And only Julie. I can't tell you how many times Scott has complained about yet another cat scratch."

"Well, Garvey will become the negotiating point, I'm betting. Though maybe it's better if Scott gets the cat?"

The impish look on Aimi's face wore away Jackson's remaining doubts. He definitely wanted to know her better. A lot better. He tugged gently on her ear, pleased when she leaned toward him. "Looks like someone's got a mean streak," he said.

"Only when others bring it out in me."

"Remind me never to get on that side of you, then."

"Smart choice," Aimi said.

Dana and Josh joined them at that point and Josh handed Jackson a mug of coffee.

"Oh, that reminds me. I called that attorney about your case."

Jackson tensed. He really needed his legal problem to go away. "How did it go?"

She looked at Josh. "Should we should talk about this at the office?"

"Dana knows all about it and Jackson and I are personally involved, so talking here is fine," Josh said.

"All right. Well, I'd plunk that attorney soundly in the shyster category."

"That doesn't sound good."

"There's good and bad. The case isn't going to just disappear but someone like that is always willing to settle out of court."

"Jackson didn't do anything wrong," Dana said.

"We all know he didn't," Josh validated. "Which means there's no reason we should settle."

"I agree," Jackson said. No way did he want to settle a frivolous lawsuit. It would set a precedent.

"Settling makes it all go away."

"That grates right up against my sense of right and wrong. I protected that kid. Taught him a lesson and kept him safe until his parents found him. Heck, he wouldn't give me his name or tell me where they were staying. What the hell else was I supposed to do?" Jackson ran a hand over his short hair.

"You did everything right," Aimi said. "It's a tough pill to swallow, but some people just don't see anything wrong with their kids and they'll fight tooth and nail if they think the child has been harmed, physically or emotionally." Aimi took a deep breath. "That's where I think these parents are and they probably just want to be heard. From what the attorney said, the boy may have enhanced the story. Played up his fright."

"They believe him over me." Jackson sank back into the couch, defeated.

"Right. Look, normally I would say let's settle."

When Jackson stiffened again, she held up her hand.

"Correct me if I'm wrong, but what you really want is for the parents to understand that their son committed a crime and they need to deal with that."

"I'd be happy with that."

"Then I suggest we not settle and let the case go to mediation. You, and Willow Bay, will sit across a table from them and get to tell your story."

"That sounds perfect."

"As you know, though, any agreement reached through mediation will be final. You may have to agree to pay restitution if you want this resolved quickly."

"Willow Bay's liability insurance will cover it. Whatever they don't cover, the city will," Josh chimed in. "You've done a lot for Willow Bay, Jackson. We've got your back."

"Thank you. All right, I say let's go to mediation."

"I second that," Josh said.

"I'll set it up."

"Good," Dana said. "Now that that's all decided, let's get those steaks on the grill and get this dinner going."

Everyone stood and prepared to go through the kitchen to the back deck.

"Wait," Jackson said to Aimi. "If you're uncomfortable with me here, I can leave."

"No. I'm not." She took a deep breath and gazed at him. "You confuse me, Jackson."

"How?" He cocked his head.

"I'm attracted to you."

"I like this so far."

"Let me finish. I'm attracted to you at a time when I have no business being attracted to anyone. A relationship, right now, is the furthest thing from my mind."

"Why? Because of your fledgling business? Folks in Willow Bay won't hold dating the town sheriff against you. Might even bolster their opinion of you."

"Except you're my client. And that's not the only thing."

He held his breath, hoping he'd get something, anything, to understand why she was so skittish.

"I'm an emotional wreck, Jackson. My job in Spokane, along with other pressures, has wrung me out. I need to get my feet back underneath me before I can consider a relationship, even the friends-with-benefits kind."

Damn. Kind of hard to argue that one. He reached for her, frowning when she stepped back and hugged herself. Well, shoot. Time to put on the patience cap and ratchet it down tight.

Jackson stepped back as well. "I like you, Aimi. I'll admit that makes me nervous because I've seen too many couples fail. But I think we're worth a try. We have chemistry." *Lots of chemistry.* "However, if we're not in the same place at the same time, I can be patient."

Aimi's arms dropped and her shoulders relaxed. The smile she gave him cemented his belief that he'd made the right choice. Though the wait would not be easy, he already knew she was worth it. But he'd need to be really patient. Not his strongest suit.

"Thank you, Jackson."

"I already respect you, Aimi. Know that. I can be a friend."

She nodded and went to pass him.

"For now," he said to her back, stopping her in her tracks. "Though I can't promise I won't remind you every once in a while that there's something more between us waiting to be explored. I hope one day you'll learn to trust me."

She didn't turn around. He thought she might not answer. When she did, he almost missed it, she was so quiet.

"I want to."

She fled to the kitchen, leaving him wondering again why she found it hard to trust. Letting that thought go, he walked in to find her and Dana absorbed in salad prep, so he topped off his coffee, grabbed a beer for Josh, and headed out to the deck where his friend stood guard over the barbeque.

"Did you bring me a beer?"

"You bet." Jackson handed it over and leaned against the house near where Josh grilled.

"So, you and Aimi, huh?"

Jackson shook his head. "I don't think so."

"Really? I thought there was a spark there."

"You're right, at least as far as I'm concerned, but something's got her gun shy."

"Before you ask, I don't know anything specific. And, bro code or not, it wouldn't be my story to tell."

"Just answer me this. Was she abused?"

"No. At least, not to my knowledge."

"Thank goodness."

"Yeah."

"What are you two doing looking so serious out here?" Dana set dishes on the deck table while Aimi put down a salad bowl, along with a bottle of wine.

"Just solving world problems, as most men do," Josh answered.

"Oh! If I thought you actually believed that, I'd take you to task over it," Dana said.

Josh laughed and Dana kissed him, lingering in a very personal and married way. It filled Jackson with melancholy. All of a sudden, he wanted that. He shouldn't. He knew better. Glancing at Aimi, he could see stark desire in her eyes, too. Her lips pursed, pouty and perfect, and it took everything Jackson had not to claim that mouth as his own.

Jackson sipped his coffee and vowed to change Aimi's mind, even if it meant they could only be friends—with no benefits—for a while. It might frustrate him, but he'd do it. Something about her captivated him, even though he usually wasn't interested in relationships. Experience had taught him they just didn't work out. Which is why he didn't understand how, after so short a time, he was in so deep with this woman, or how he knew he wanted to follow this attraction through to the end.

And take a whole lot of cold showers in the interim.

~~~

"So what's up with you and Jackson?" Dana loaded glasses and silverware on her tray.

"What do you mean?"

"I mean, I thought you two were hot for each other."

"Maybe, but I'm not ready."

Dana pulled Aimi in for a quick hug. "You can't let the past determine the arc for your future, Aimi. Jackson's a good man."

"I know that. He's also a strong man. What I don't trust is my ability to hold the force of him at bay and remain my own person."

"I vouch for him. So does Josh."

"A lot of people do, apparently. Still doesn't get through my thick skin. I need to do this in my own time."

"All right. I can see by the defiant tilt of your head that I'd better back off. Take these out. I'll get the bread out of the oven, cut it, and join you. The steaks should be about done."

Aimi took the tray outside and set the table, trying not to glance at Jackson but unable to stop herself. She caught him staring at her, a bemused expression on his face.

"Who's ready for steaks?" Josh said, piling them on a plate and turning the barbeque off.

"I am," Dana said coming through the door. "Perfect timing. The bread is done."

Through the first part of dinner, Dana and Josh carried the conversation. Jackson looked deep in thought and Aimi was too busy trying to sort out her own muddled emotions.
~~~

But, by the time they'd all piled their plates high, Jackson had joined the conversation and pulled Aimi in with him. When she pushed away from the table, she leaned back and held her stomach.

"I ate way too much," she said.

"Me, too." Jackson tried to jiggle his non-existent belly fat.

They all laughed.

"I hope you saved room for dessert."

Both Jackson and Josh perked up, making them all laugh again.

"Bottomless pits, these two," Dana said.

"Look who's talking, Dana," Aimi said. "I swear, it's like you're eating for two. Or three."

Dana glanced at Josh, who grinned.

"Well, I am, actually."

"You— Wait. What?"

"I'm pregnant. Why else would I turn down wine at dinner?"

Aimi squealed and leaped up to hug her friend. "I'm so happy for you."

Jackson reached over and shook Josh's hand. "Congrats, man."

"This is such a surprise," Aimi said. "I didn't know you were trying."

"We weren't, exactly. I'd call it a happy accident, but there's no way we could consider this baby anything but loved and eagerly expected."

Though she didn't let go of Dana's hand, Aimi sat back down. "I should have done more of the work tonight. You shouldn't be doing so much."

Dana laughed. "I can do whatever I would normally do. But I'll admit," she leaned toward Aimi, "I'm totally using it to get out of jogging on the beach with Josh."

"I knew that was a bogus excuse," he said, fake huffing.

Everyone laughed some more, and the discussion revolved around babies and nurseries and shopping trips until Josh stood.

"You look beat, honey," he said to Dana. "I'll do dishes."

"I'll help," Aimi said.

"I'll clear the table," Jackson said, grabbing plates.

"What will I do?" Dana asked.

"Sit," they all said in unison.

A half-hour later, the dishes were done and Aimi said her goodbyes.

"I'll walk out with you," Jackson offered.

No. Aimi bit back the word. Being alone with Jackson was too problematic. He was a hard man to resist and if he pushed even a little bit, she'd forget her resolve and fall into his arms.

She missed her chance to avoid it. Jackson put a hand to her waist and ushered her outside. At her car, he opened the door after she unlocked it with the key fob.

"I had a nice time tonight," he said.

"So did I." Why did he have to smell so good?

Jackson leaned in, pecked her on the cheek, and stood back until she got in her car. True to his word, he kept it friendly. "I'll follow you home."

"No." The claustrophobia bubbled up. "I can take care of myself."

"Just to make sure you get there safe."

"No, thank you. Please don't follow me."

Aimi started her car, put it in gear, and peeled out a little faster than she'd planned. She thought about her old office, the times she was held back for promotion, how often she'd been told she should go out with so-and-so because it would be good for her career. Orders, that's what they'd been. She'd quit so she didn't have to take those orders, and now here she was. She would not let a man dictate to her ever again.

Halfway home and with no other vehicle in her rearview mirror, Aimi began to relax, which made her think about that friendly peck on the cheek. She'd almost turned her head. The need to kiss him was growing inside her and she didn't know how long she could hold out against his charm. She wanted him, body, mind, and soul. She just didn't want to be under his thumb.

How would she resist him long enough to find herself, to become what she truly wanted to be?

Aimi got out of her car. Distracted by her thoughts, she didn't see the dark shape come at her. Before she could react, a hand grabbed at her shoulder bag. Aimi took hold of the strap of her bag and was yanked forward so fast she couldn't keep her feet under her. She went down hard on the concrete, crying out in pain as she hit.

"Stop!" she yelled at the thief, to no avail. The shadow had disappeared.

Someone heard her, though. Red and blue lights flashed as Jackson's cruiser raced into the alley and slammed to a stop behind her car. He dashed to her side.

"Are you hurt?"

"Yes. No." Aimi shook her head. "I don't know."

"I'll call the paramedics."

"No," Aimi said. "I don't need them. I'm mostly just shaken. Please, help me sit up."

Jackson wouldn't let her up until he'd felt her arms, legs, head, and neck for injuries. Once she was upright, he asked her what happened.

"Someone stole my bag. Ripped it right off my shoulder. I tried to hold on, but that only brought me down." She brushed gravel off her sore palms.

"Which way did the thief go?"

Aimi pointed over her shoulder, then moaned when the joint complained.

Jackson peered into the darkness, then back at Aimi. "Come on, let's get you inside. Do you have your keys?"

"They were in my hand, so they have to be around here somewhere."

"Stay here." Jackson scanned the pavement with his flashlight. He quickly found Aimi's keys, unlocked the back door to the shop, then helped her stand.

"Oooh, everything is starting to hurt."

"We should take you to the hospital."

"I don't need a hospital. I just need to rest."

"But— "

Inside now, with lights on so Jackson could see her face, Aimi gave him her don't-mess-with-me lawyer look.

It worked. Jackson helped her sit down on the bed then backed up, hands in the air. "Geesh, you use that look in court?"

"Works every time," she said, moving her shoulders, neck, everything she could to make sure she'd been right about what she'd told him. Didn't feel like anything was broken. She'd be sore for a while, though. Really sore.

"Your hands are a mess."

He was right. The embedded gravel and bloody scrapes looked pretty nasty and were starting to sting.

"Wait here a minute." Jackson went out into Dana's shop, returning with a wet cloth, a dry cloth, and her first aid kit.

"I can take care of these."

"That will hurt you more, moving one hand to fix the other. Let me do it. Please." He waited with extreme patience until Aimi finally held out her hands.

Jackson barely hurt her at all while cleaning the wounds, he was so gentle. Several minutes later, her palms were slathered in antibiotic ointment and wrapped in gauze.

"Now let me take a look at those elbows." He lifted her arms, one at a time. "They don't look too bad. A little road rash, but I think I can leave the cleaning to you. Your palms took the worst of it." He pulled her bandaged hands to his lips, kissing one at a time.

The gesture was so sweet, Aimi had to admit it was nice being taken care of by Jackson. He helped her lay back on the bed, covered her with the afghan that lay across the end, and put together an ice pack for her shoulder.

"Can you tell me what happened?"

She did, giving as much information as she could. Jackson asked questions, pulling details from her she hadn't remembered.

"Does this happen often around here?"

"Hardly at all." He frowned. "In fact, not in several months, so I'm surprised."

"Great."

"You don't have any enemies that might have followed you here, do you?"

A few lawyers and partners, maybe, after the way she'd left. Maybe a client's angry husband or two, but no one specific. "Not that I'm aware of."

"But you do have enemies."

"I negotiate divorce agreements. Sometimes, people are bitter, but I can't imagine they'd come after me like that. Though I didn't leave my job on the best of terms."

Damn. That was too much information. Jackson was smart and Aimi doubted he'd let that one pass by. Yet all he did was cock his head and gaze at her for a long moment.

"Did the guy get anything of value?"

"That's the funny thing. All I was carrying in that bag were leftover cleaning supplies I'd borrowed from here. My wallet wasn't even in there. The person got dirty rags and Soft-Scrub." She chuckled. "I bet he was pissed."

"You said he."

"I made an assumption. I really don't know."

"Okay." Jackson resituated the ice pack on her shoulder, leaning over her to do so.

He was so close and smelled so good. It would take nothing to kiss him. If he moved his head just slightly.

His eyes went dark as he stared into hers. Aimi gulped. She wanted to kiss him so badly she ached. When his eyes dipped to her lips, she ran her tongue across them, wanting him to close what little distance lay between them.

Then he pulled back and Aimi shivered with cold. He snugged the blanket tighter around her. "I'd better leave, or I'll be tempted to do a lot more than you want right now."

Conflicted like she'd never been before, Aimi couldn't speak. She missed his nearness. She wanted him. But she'd set the limitations, and Jackson apparently had more strength than she did.

"Are you okay?" His voice, huskier than usual, held tender care.

"Yes. Thank you for being here."

"I wasn't following you. I gave you your space, but I go right by here on my way home."

"Thank goodness."

"If I hadn't had the window rolled down... " Jackson stared over her head, lost in his own thoughts.

Aimi put a bandaged hand on his. "Don't go there. It was basically a hit and run. The thief was already racing away before you arrived."

Jackson cupped her face. "I know we're just friends right now, but if anything happened to you— "

"It didn't. I'm fine. See?" She removed the ice pack and rotated her shoulder, but not without wincing. "Okay, I'll be fine in a few days. Right now, I think I just need some sleep."

He kissed her, a light peck on the lips, then stood. "I hate to make you get up, but I can't lock the door behind me unless you want to give me your keys."

"No. No offense."

"None taken." He winked at her. Actually winked. "It's too soon."

"That lopsided grin of his was a heady weapon. Aimi almost caved.

"See me out?"

She climbed off the bed with his helping hand and followed him to the door.

"Keep your phone by you, and call me if you need anything."

"I don't take orders, Jackson." Aimi had slipped into her court voice without thought. She shouldn't have. Jackson had been nothing but helpful and caring. Another reason why she didn't do relationships. Too much guessing. Too much rethinking her own gut reactions.

He gave her an exasperated look. "Please."

She nodded. He tugged a lock of her hair and was gone.

Aimi locked the door and leaned against it, already missing him. Damn it. What would it be like dating Jackson Smith? Probably full of nothing but fights. Aimi smiled. Fights could be fun, though. Maybe it was time to lift her moratorium on relationships. Maybe she should give Jackson a chance.

Maybe she shouldn't make decisions in this mood. Aimi hobbled to the bathroom, giving in to the aches and pains. Time for some ibuprofen, then bed.

And dreams. Too many dreams, all including one very hot sheriff.

~~~

Jackson pulled his cruiser around to the front of Tangerine Treasures and got out. He checked all the stores. Nothing looked amiss. He walked around to the back and took pictures of the boot prints leading away from Aimi's car. Well-spaced prints, so she'd probably been right that it was a male. They headed up the sand dune and straight for the beach. He'd lose the tracks in the grassy dune, so not much sense trying to follow the perp, especially not in the dark. Nothing moved other than the willow and grass swaying in the slight wind.

Frustrated, he went back to his cruiser and headed home. It went against everything he believed in to leave Aimi there alone. She was stubborn and he couldn't force the issue, so he'd give her the lead. But damn, it bothered him, her there all alone after something like this.

He'd call her in the morning to make sure she'd done okay overnight. That was all he could do for now. Jackson tried to tell himself he was taking care of her like he would anyone from Willow Bay. A big fat lie.

For a moment, he wondered what it would be like, being married to her. Having her in his bed every night, eating meals together, talking about their days. He couldn't shake how much he liked the idea.

Getting out of his car and heading into his sparsely furnished, newly purchased home, Jackson pulled out his phone and called his youngest sister.

"Hey, Jordan."

"Jackson! This is a nice surprise. What's wrong?"

"Nothing. I thought I'd see how you're doing."

"Jackson, you have two sisters and you never call either of us unless you need to talk. What's up?"

"Honestly, everything is good here. I just wanted to hear your voice. You doing okay?"
~~~

"I'm doing fine. So's your nephew. He got the birthday card you sent him and immediately plunked the money into his piggy bank. He's saving for an X-Box. Won't take him long with what you send him."

Jackson shrugged for no one's benefit but his own. "I don't see him often enough, so if I can help him find something fun to do, I'm in."

"You may not see him much, but you spoil him anyhow."

"Isn't an uncle supposed to do that?"

Jordan laughed and Jackson realized her lilting laughter was a lot like Aimi's.

"I talked to Julie. That lawyer you had call her really made her feel better. She's more empowered now."

"Good. She's got the guts to take Scott on. She just needed to find them."

"I agree. So, this attorney. You seeing her?"

"Nope." He needed to put the kibosh on that thought right away. "How about you? Seeing anyone?"

"No. Steve... Well, Steve cured me of men for a long while."

"I wish he hadn't dumped you like that. I could have talked to him."

"What good would talking to him do? He didn't break the law. He just broke my heart."

"It would have made me feel better, especially if he'd ended up with a black eye or two."

"You'd be in jail and Ethan wouldn't have an uncle padding his X-box fund." Jordan laughed. "Seriously, bro, I'm okay and happy with my life. I'm just not interested in dating yet."

"I get it." Jackson pulled a cold beer out of the fridge and opened it, sitting on a counter stool.

"We've all had broken hearts," Jordan said. "They take a while to mend."

"How long, though? How long does it take to get over some asshole like Steve?"

"You asking for me or for yourself? Did some woman crush your heart, Jackson?"

"No. It's not like that."

"But you're seeing someone."

"I'd like to, but she's skittish."

"Ahhh, so you *do* want to date the attorney, and you need advice."

He really hated when his sister saw through him like this. She was right. Among the siblings, she had the coolest head on her shoulders. Plus, she'd finished school and had become a counselor. Seemed wise to call her on those rare occasions when he needed help.

"I don't know how to help her get past whatever's holding her back, Jordan."

"The tough part is, you can't get her past it. All you can do is give her time and see if she works through it. Be her friend."

"Not the answer I was looking for."

Jordan laughed. "I know. It's the right one, though."

"Yeah. I guess." Jackson sighed and took a pull on his beer. "Means my instincts are right. Time and patience."

"Lots of it."

"Thanks, sis."

"Anytime, bro. One of these days, you need to fly home and visit."

"I know. I will. Right now, things are unsettled."

"Well, once they get settled, come visit. We want to hear all about the woman who brought the big man down."

Jackson ended the call to the pleasant sound of Jordan's laughter. He stared at his cell phone, knowing she was right. Time and patience.

He only prayed he had enough of both to wait for Aimi.

CHAPTER NINE

Aimi rolled over and groaned. Everything hurt. Her palms stung beneath the bandages, and her shoulder ached like the dickens. Hell, everything ached. All from one toss to the ground? Ugh.

Sitting up with as much care as she could, dizziness assailed her and she had to wait a couple minutes for it to pass. Had she hit her head? No, Jackson had palpated and found no lumps. Maybe she was just groggy. Fumbling with bandaged hands, she turned the light on, then checked the time on her phone. Wow, 9:45? No wonder she was stiff and groggy. She never slept this late.

Dana would be here soon and Aimi had fallen asleep in last night's clothes. She needed to change. But she also needed a shower, and help getting her bandages off. While she didn't want to worry Dana with the story, it looked like she needed a little help.

The bells chimed at the front of the shop. Dana had arrived. And she must have seen Aimi's lights on, because in moments she stood in the doorway.

"You're still here?" Dana said, then gasped when Aimi held up her bandaged hands.

"What happened?"

"Some jerk as I came home last night. Threw me to the ground and took off with the bag I had over my shoulder."

"Oh, gosh, he got your purse?"

"No." Aimi laughed. "Just your cleaning supplies. I borrowed them for the office and was bringing them home."

"Good. I hope that pissed the guy off big time. Your poor hands."

"And shoulder, and well, everything hurts, to be quite honest."

"That's it. You're coming to live with us."

"Absolutely not."

"It's not safe here anymore."

"Sure it is. This was just one incident. And a rare one, according to Jackson."

"Jackson came back here with you?" Dana's eyebrows shot up.

"No. He was driving by and heard me yell."

"Well, I'm thankful for that. I wish you'd give him a chance, Aims."

"I'm not ready."

"He's not like the guys you worked with. He's not that asshole who tried to force himself on you in the women's room. Jackson is different."

"I took care of that restroom problem pretty well, you know."

Dana huffed out a laugh. "Yes, with a knee to the crotch. But that was enough to mess with your head. Jackson's sweet. He'd never force you to do anything."

He already is. Aimi just couldn't seem to stop thinking about the man.

"I get the feeling he likes to take charge and give orders."

"He's the sheriff!"

"I just... I'm not ready, okay? Jackson understands that and he's giving me the time I need to... adapt."

"You don't look particularly pleased with that."

"Well, have you taken a good look at him? He's hot as sin, and he smells so good. Every time I get near him, my resolve weakens."

"Then why not give in?"

"Not until I'm ready." Aimi straightened. "Now, can you help me take these bandages off? I want to take a shower."

After she finished, Aimi put antibiotic salve on her palms again, but fixed a much smaller bandage so she could use her hands better. She heard someone talking to Dana in the shop and leaned against the closed door to listen to Jackson's rich, deep voice.

Aimi wasn't even dressed. If he knocked on the door... She raced around, tossing on clothes as fast as her aching muscles would allow. Her phone pinged just as she slipped into sandals.

Are you up? I stopped by to see how you're feeling this morning.

Jackson. Aimi smiled. Caring, but giving her the space she'd asked for. Could he be any nicer?

Yes. I'll be out in a moment.

She brushed her hair, unable to wipe the grin off her face. When her phone pinged again, she thought it was Jackson.

I know where you live.

What? The text came from an unknown phone number. Aimi sank onto her bed.

Who is this?

You'll find out. You ruined my life. Now, I'm going to ruin yours.

With shaking hands, she tossed the phone on her bed. Who the hell?

At a small tap on her door, Aimi started. Working hard to calm herself, she opened it.

"Hi, Jackson." Good. Barely any quaver to her voice.

His smile was tentative. He reached for her, then pulled back. "Are you all right?"

"I'm f-fine."

"Really?"

"Sore. But otherwise, none the worse." She closed her eyes briefly at the lie. "Look. I redressed my hands."

He took both of them, inspecting. "Any redness around the edges?"

"No. I took a shower and I think all my road rash is doing better already, thanks to you. I put on more ointment." She wiggled her fingers.

Jackson pulled her hands to his chest, causing her to step closer. He lifted a lock of her hair. "I like your hair down like this."

Just that one simple statement and Aimi never wanted to put her hair up or in clips again.

You ruined my life. Now I'm going to ruin yours.

Who had texted her? And was it some sort of practical joke or a real threat? Aimi didn't believe in coincidences. After last night, then this, she didn't think it was a joke. Still, she needed time to sort this out. She should tell Jackson. He'd help her. And more than likely, he'd do what he needed to do to protect her, way more than she could handle at the moment. Until she could sort this out and figure out who had sent these texts, there wasn't much he could do. With fear and regret clogging her throat, she pulled her hair from his hand and backed away.

She needed distance. Time to think. "I need to get to the office."

"Do you have clients other than me?"

"Maybe."

He eyed her for so long that Aimi had to suppress the urge to come clean. Impressive, but she'd cut her legal teeth on that maneuver and had learned the stare, which she gave right back to him.

But Jackson wasn't one to back down without a fight. "Work can wait. You're injured."

"Work never stops when you have your own business. And my hands are much better this morning."

"And your shoulder?"

She rotated her shoulder, happy she managed only a slight wince even though it hurt like a son-of-a-bitch. "Almost back to normal."

"Hmm. I'm betting that hurts more than you're letting on. Let me drive you to work."

"No." She said the word fast.

His eyes narrowed. "What's going on, Aimi?"

When he stepped through the doorway toward her, she held up her hand. "Not right now, Jackson. I have some things to take care of, and I can get myself to the office. I'm grateful for your help last night, but I've got this."

Aimi tried to shield herself against the hurt in his eyes, but the knife slithered into her heart anyhow. Damn. This wasn't easy, keeping him at arm's length.

"No problem. I've got the message loud and clear."

Jackson turned on his heel and left as quickly as he could. Aimi stood in the bedroom doorway and watched him go, regret and resolve at war inside her. She'd tell him. Soon. After she gained a measure of control over the situation.

Dana, busy checking out a customer at the counter in the shot, glanced at Aimi with concern on her face. Which meant Aimi would be grilled shortly. Instead of facing it, she grabbed her purse and keys and, like the coward she was, slipped out the back door.

On the short, painful drive to her office, she spent as much time watching her rear-view mirror as she did the road ahead. Once there, she had to try the door key three times, owing to her damaged and trembling hands. Inside, she locked the door behind her and left the closed sign in the window.

Heading to her desk in the still-dark office, she hit something with a thunk.

"Ow." Aimi backtracked and turned on the lights.

A chair in the middle of the room? When had she moved that there? Aimi thought through the last time she'd been here and how she'd locked up. An ice-cold dread shivered down her spine. She hadn't moved the chair.

And if she hadn't moved it, who had?

~~~

Jackson spent the next couple of hours going about his business, his mind on Aimi every chance it got. Something had happened to her between last night and this morning. She'd changed. Gone cold. And damn it, she wouldn't tell him a thing. He wanted to shake it out of her even if that wasn't his style. She needed to tell him in her own time. But his patience was growing thin. He'd driven by the office three times in the last hour. Her car was there, but the closed sign stayed put.

Why?

He stopped by Dana's shop.

"Have you seen Aimi?" he asked.

"Not since this morning. After you left, she lit out of here so fast I didn't even have time to say goodbye."

"Did something upset her?"

"Not that I know of. I helped her out of the bandages, she took a shower, and you showed up." Dana eyed him. "What did you two talk about? Did you fight?"
~~~

"We didn't have time to fight. She shut me down so fast, it blindsided me."

"Then something happened between my time with her and you," Dana said, pointing between them.

Jackson ran his hands over his head. "I have no idea what. Maybe she got a call or text from someone in Spokane?"

Dana's eyebrows rose. "I can't imagine who. She tidied up there before heading out. She didn't want anything following her."

"What did she need to tidy up? What happened to her, Dana? Why does she back away whenever I try to get close to her?"

No response. Dana only wrung her hands together.

"Something's wrong. She wouldn't leave here like that," Jackson said. "And if you have information that will help me help her, you need to tell me."

"It's not my story to tell."

"Damn it. She won't tell me. You've got to give me something."

"Fine. She had an issue with a guy. Someone she worked with."

Jackson saw red. "Did he hurt her?"

"No."

"She could have lied about that."

"I don't think she did. She mentioned that she kneed the guy in the groin."

Knowing that Aimi had taken care of herself did nothing to lessen Jackson's anger. "Who attacked her and exactly what did he do?"

"You'll have to ask her." Dana held up her hand. "Sorry, but like I said. It's her story. However, she made it clear why she was leaving and tied up every loose end so she wouldn't have to go back. That should tell you something."

"All right. I'm going to go by her office again and see if she's there."

"What if she's not?" Dana chewed her lip.

Unlike his insides, which were churning, Jackson outwardly stepped into comfort mode by adopting a casual stance and showing Dana a hint of a smile. "This is Aimi we're talking about. Wherever she is, it's exactly where she wants to be, right?"

Dana took the bait, a tremulous smile filtering in.

"So we'll cross bridges when we come to them, not before," Jackson said in his most reassuring voice.

"Let me know when you find her, okay?"

"I will."

Jackson strode out to his car, worried about Aimi and also angry. Something had happened—something she didn't want to tell him—related to her life in Spokane, which he now knew hadn't been the safest. Damn, damn, and double damn.

He left the sirens and lights off, but flew down Main Street, peeling around the corner. Her car was still parked in front of the office but the closed sign still glared at him from the window. Looking around, he noticed another car. He automatically cataloged the vehicle. Lexus SUV. Silver. Dave Smith Motors around the license plate. Probably not a local, if he bought the car in Idaho. Someone sat behind the wheel but had a hat on, so Jackson couldn't get a read on any characteristics. Hell, he couldn't even tell if the person was male or female.

He glanced at the door, then back at the car. Deciding on the car first, he took two steps toward it before it took off in a hurry, narrowly missing him in the process. And damn it. He still didn't see who was driving. The SUV swerved around the corner and disappeared. Too late to follow it. Besides, Jackson had bigger problems he needed resolved right now.

He tried the front door of Aimi's office. Locked. He knocked. No answer. Next, he pounded. Still no answer. "Aimi, if you're in there, open the damn door," he yelled. "If you don't, I'm breaking it down."

Through an interminable pause, he waited, almost sinking with relief when she responded.

"You wouldn't dare."

"Do you doubt me?"

Another pause, then the door opened. "No." She glanced down the street.

"The car is gone. Who was in the car, Aimi?"

She locked the door behind him and slumped into a reception chair, her face white as a sheet. "There was a car?"

His impatience was getting the better of him. This story was coming out in bits and pieces and he'd about had it with that. He needed answers. Since he knew from experience Aimi would shut up, or worse, run if he pushed her too hard, he went to her small fridge and pulled out a couple bottles of water, opening one and handing it to her.

"Drink."

Aimi scowled at him, which was markedly better than the previous fear she'd displayed.

"Please."

She took a couple sips, reverting right back to staring at the floor after each one.

Jackson opened his own bottle, went behind the receptionist's desk, and sat down. He waited, though it killed him. He knew what scared looked like. Aimi was spooked. He wanted to put his arms around her and tell her it would be all right, but he stayed put. "Aimi, look at me."

For once, she did.

"There's about six feet and a desk between us. I won't move from this spot, but you have to tell me what's going on. I'm going to text Dana that you're all right because she's as worried about you as I am, then we're going to talk."

CHAPTER TEN

Aimi glared at Jackson. "You ordering me, sheriff?"

"Yes. Dana is worried. I'm worried." His words, spoken with quiet intensity, killed her anger. That she'd worried her best friend bothered Aimi. A lot. She and Dana had seen each other through thick and thin and it wasn't fair to her friend to do this.

She took a drink of her water and leaned forward, settling her elbows on her knees. "Honestly, there's not much in the way of facts I can tell you."

"Just tell me from the beginning. Let me decide what's fact and what's muddied."

With a deep sigh, she began. "I think someone's after me."

Jackson opened his mouth, then closed it. Aimi had to give him props for waiting.

"I got a text this morning." She pulled her phone out of her back pocket and swiped through to the text, then handed it to Jackson.

He read it, then quickly looked up at Aimi, worry in his eyes. She knew that worry, but the fact that Jackson felt the same chilled her to the bone.

"Who sent this?" he asked.

"I don't know." Aimi took her phone back and sank into the reception chair.

"There's no phone number attached to the text, which means whoever sent it probably did so anonymously."

"I didn't even know that could be done."

Jackson nodded, his lips tight.

"Is there a way to track something like this?" Aimi asked. Wasn't that something cooked up by cop shows?

"Not that I'm aware of. Besides, this is way beyond anything we can do here. We send everything out to the state."

"Then it's a dead end." Aimi got up and started to pace.

Jackson crumpled his water bottle, the sound of crunching plastic filling the room. He tossed it with a little too much force into the trash bin. It bounced out, a perfect reminder that things were not going Aimi's way.

"I may know a guy," he said. "If there's a way to track this, he'd know."

While he made the call, Aimi went into her office. She might as well try to get some work done, though focusing wasn't her strong point at the moment.

"Well, that was a bust," Jackson said, joining her after a few minutes. "It can be done, but it takes more time and resources than we can muster."

"Damn." She thrummed her fingers on the desk.

I'm going to put in a request to state to take a look at this, just to get in the queue while we try to sort this out." Sitting on the desk, Jackson picked up Aimi's hand, careful of her scrapes as he ran his thumb across the top of it. A small movement, but it meant a lot to her. She wasn't alone. He'd help her figure this out. Jackson calmed her.

"I don't want to pry," he said in his quiet voice. "But could this have anything to do with why you left your job in Spokane?"

Aimi tensed. So much for calming down. "I doubt it."

"I can't help you if I don't have all the facts. Why did you move here, Aimi?"

She pulled her hand from his and scooted her chair back, needing room. "Look, that can't be related to today's threat. Nothing that serious happened at the office." She waved at her phone. "Nothing worth this level of menace."

Jackson moved to the other side of the desk and sat down, remaining quiet. This time, Aimi folded first, sighing heavily.

"Fine. Look, I got tired of the testosterone party going on where I worked. I was told that if I worked hard, I'd make partner in a few short years. But every time a promotion became available, they handed it to one of the guys. Turned out, they needed a token woman to appear progressive."

"That had to be frustrating."

"It was."

He cocked his head. "But I can't imagine it's the reason you left town. You'd take that as a challenge."

Oh, God, how could he know her so well already? Aimi shook her head. "You're right. I'd pretty much accepted the challenge, right up until a lawyer hired only three months earlier got promoted after we won a big case. A case I'd worked on for a solid year. He came in at the end and took all the credit—and a surprise promotion."

"Even then, I wasn't planning to leave the area, though I'd started putting feelers out for another job." She looked off into the distance.

"What changed your mind?"

"The new guy cornered me. In the ladies' room, of all places. Tried to sweet talk me into a quickie. When that didn't work, he got more… forceful."

Jackson's hands clenched the sides of his chair, but he didn't move. Another plus in his column.

"I kneed him in the groin. Hard. He crumpled to the floor and I marched myself right up to the managing partners' offices, where they were all meeting, and lodged a complaint. My blouse was torn, but they didn't care. They said outright that I'd probably led him on."

She'd hated that day, realizing that she couldn't break through old-guard bias, at least not at that firm. She'd spent the next few hours bouncing between anger and her first-ever brush with futility. She'd talked to Dana and decided to file charges against the firm.

"You didn't file charges, did you?"

"I was going to. I went back the next morning to find my office cleared out and my cases reassigned. Some of those cases were pretty sensitive and I knew damn well they wouldn't be handled the way they should. So instead of filing charges, I went home and called all my clients with open cases, warning them that I'd been fired and they might not have the kind of representation they should have. By the end of that day, I was served with a cease-and-desist order. That's when I decided it was time to leave Spokane. Dana had been trying to get me to move here for months and it seemed like a good opportunity."

"So that's it? No one pays for treating you the way they did?"

"Oh, no. I don't roll over quite that easily. I filed a complaint with the Bar Association and the Equal Opportunity Employment Commission. The Bar Association will be deposing Dana and me next month. And

I sent pictures with the complaint, of the torn blouse, which I still have. And of the bruises on my arms."

Jackson leaped up, his tight fists white. "Bruises?" His voice, low and deadly, got Aimi's attention. She came around the desk and placed a hand on his arm.

"It's all right. My injuries weren't too bad and they healed quickly." She reached for his fist, coaxed him into relaxing it, then cupped it to her cheek. "I'm all right, Jackson." She used the same quiet voice he had, trying to prove to him that she really was all right. "No marks, no injuries, no lasting effects."

His other hand came up until her face was cocooned in his gentle grip. His thumb caressed her cheek. "You don't deserve to be treated like that, Aimi Larson."

"No woman does."

"True, but especially you. From what little I know of you, you fight like a bulldog for the vulnerable. You are a beautiful, sensitive, and caring person."

His eyes were dark, shining pools of emotion and Aimi couldn't think, couldn't act. All she could do was stare and get lost in them. In him. When he lowered his head, the kiss seemed like the most natural thing in the world. The way his lips feathered along hers soothed her, calmed her, gave her the peace of knowing she wasn't alone.

The kiss deepened, his lips claiming hers. Aimi reached her arms up around his neck, pulling him in closer, needing more. Needing all of him. She opened to him, reveling in the feel of his tongue and hers, dancing, sending sparks thrumming through her body. He pulled her in tight against his hardness, tipped her back, and kissed his way to her throat. Aimi leaned back further giving him access. More. She needed more. Her hand reached for him and he jerked beneath her.

Suddenly, he raised his head.

"What?" she asked, her voice husky with desire.

"Your phone is ringing," Jackson said.

Her phone? She hadn't even heard it, but she did now.

"Let it go to voicemail," she said, but, sensing that the mood had shifted, she sighed and reached for it. "Hello?" She moved back around her desk and sat in her chair, wishing she could fan the flames that engulfed her body.

"Aimi?" the female voice said.

"Yes, this is Aimi." Distracted by the distinct bulge Jackson was trying to resituate, she didn't immediately recognize the voice.

"It's Helen. Helen Smoots."

Smoots. Aimi dug through her muddled brain for the name. Oh, client. Rough case. She'd helped Helen escape her abusive husband before she got their divorce finalized.

"How are you doing Helen? Is everything all right?"

"I'm fine. The new start you helped me find has been amazing. But that's not what I'm calling about. I think you might be in danger, and I think I'm the reason."

That wasn't what Aimi had expected to hear. She punched the speaker button and set her phone on the desk, trying to still her shaking hands. "Helen, the sheriff happens to be here with me. Would it be all right if he listened in? And told him a little bit about your situation?"

"Yes, of course."

"So, why do you think I'm in danger? Your ex-husband?"

"Yes."

Shit. Aimi remembered him now. Monty Smoots. He'd screamed at her outside the courthouse. Came at her. If there hadn't been security guards there, he might have gotten to her. "You don't have any contact with him, do you?"

"None at all, but I heard a couple things through the grapevine."

Aimi had helped Helen get away through a group that helped abused families. "You're not supposed to have any contact with anyone from your life in Spokane."

"I know, but, well, I missed JoEllen."

"Your best friend?"

"Yes, so I reached out to her. Just once, to give her my new email address. She goes to the library to email me, never from home. And she's planning to join me here as soon as she finishes her doctorate."

The two always had been close. "I'm glad you'll have someone with you."

"Me, too, and I know it's dangerous to call you, but I had to warn you."

"Sheriff here. What do you need to warn Aimi about?" Jackson asked.

"Monty has disappeared from Spokane. Before he left, he was making a lot of noise about somebody needing to pay for him losing me."

"How do you know he left Spokane?"

"No one at the bar he frequents—my friend has friends that work there—has seen him in days."

"Maybe he took a fishing trip? Or camping?" Jackson said.

"No, listen. The night before he disappeared, he was drunk in that bar. Said again that someone was going to pay, then said 'that lawyer gal is going down.'"

Aimi clutched hands that would not stop shaking.

"How long has he been gone?" Jackson asked.

"About three days."

Long enough to get here and reconnoiter. Damn it. Aimi moved her hands to her lap.

"Is there anything else you can tell us?" she asked Helen.

"Not that I can think of. I'm just glad you still had your same cell number so I could warn you."

"Thank you, Helen. I hope this call doesn't put you in danger."

"My friend's going to join me at the end of the month. We'll be moving and not telling anyone where."

"Good. Stay safe, and have a happy life, Helen. You deserve it."

"You be safe, too. I'm sorry, Aimi. I wish this wasn't happening."

"Not your fault." Aimi took a deep breath. "And I've got friends here. People who will help me stay safe." She lifted her chin. "I'll be fine."

"I'll have this cell number until the thirtieth," Helen said. "So call me if you can and let me know how you are."

"I will."

After disconnecting, Aimi sat and stared at the phone. Jackson came around the desk and pulled her up into his arms. "We'll find this guy, Aimi. We'll keep you safe."

Tears stung her eyes. She'd always fought her own battles and could be fierce in the courtroom, but right now, having Jackson's help eased her fears. Jackson was a good man, and good at his job. He'd help her with everything he had. She felt that in her soul. But could she trust him with her heart?

Aimi sank into him, letting her frustration and fear fall in unwanted tears. Her arms wrapped around him as his own tightened. "Thank you, Jackson."

She'd never needed help until now, but by God, she was going to accept it. Having someone after her like this was way beyond her purview, and Aimi was more than grateful Jackson was here.

It took way too long for Aimi to get herself together and pull back. "I never cry. Certainly never like that."

Jackson chuckled. "You needed to."

"I'll be back in a minute. Just going to freshen up."

"I'll be right here."

In the small bathroom, Aimi glanced in the mirror. *Oh, my God. I look like the Stay-Puft Marshmallow Man.* She wasn't wearing makeup, her eyes were red, and her cheeks and under-eyes were puffy. Her straight, dark hair was a tangled mess. She turned on the water and splashed some over her face, blotting it dry with paper towels. It didn't help much.

"You don't look as bad as you think." Jackson's voice came from the other side of the door. "Let's just rip the Band-Aid off, shall we?" He opened the door quickly, giving her no option to refuse.

"Jackson!"

"What?"

"I'm in the ladies' room."

He looked at the door. "Looks unisex to me."

"But what if… What if I— "

"Were peeing? I've seen it before."

Aimi's eyes were about as wide as they could get. "Not from me, you haven't."

"We'll just have to do something to remedy that." Again, giving her no chance to turn him down, Jackson moved into her space, cupped her neck in his hand, his other one settling on her hip, and lowered his lips to hers.

Shock gave way to sensation. He took charge, delved in, but with sweet tenderness. Aimi pushed at his lips with her tongue and he gave way. Together, they fanned the fire growing within them. Already blazing, if Aimi was any judge as Jackson pressed her tight against him. Seconds, minutes, hours. Who knew how much time passed? Aimi gave herself over to the sheer pleasure and rampant desire that raced through her.

When Jackson pulled away and leaned back against the wall, they were both breathing hard.

"Just wanted you to forget your troubles for a little while," he said, with that sexy smile that always made her melt.

She ran her fingers over his lips. "Boy, did you." She reached in for more, but Jackson set himself back.

"If we do any more, we'll be testing that couch in your office. And, sweetheart?" He cupped her face and gave her a quick kiss on the lips. "When we do this—and it is when, not if—we're going to take our time and enjoy ourselves."

Aimi's core clenched as his words, deep and assured, echoed through her.

"All right," she finally said, still working to find her equilibrium. "But no more kisses like that until we're in the right place. At the right time. And we have all night."

His dark eyes glittered. "No guarantees. I like kissing you. A lot. But, since this is neither the time nor the place, I'll leave you to what you were doing." He started to close the door, then opened it again. "And I won't barge in this time."

Once the door was closed, Aimi slumped onto the toilet seat, completely spent. Between the crying and the kissing, every ounce of energy had leached out of her body. Wow. What a roller coaster. And what a way to finish.

She joined Jackson a few minutes later. He flashed his thousand-watt smile at her, inviting her closer and putting an arm around her waist while he talked on the phone. After he hung up, he tipped her head this way and that. "No evidence of tears, and I'm an expert on evidence." He took a deep breath. "But, reality intrudes. Dana just called. Someone spray-painted the back door to the shop."

"With what? Did it say something?"

Jackson's lips tightened.

"No secrets. If you start holding out on me, you won't be the one helping me solve this."

With a brief nod, he told her the spray-painted words: "You're dead."

Oh, shit. Aimi sank against her desk.

"I think we need to put him on notice that you're not alone. I've asked Josh and Dana to meet us at the police station to talk about this. Bernie and her husband, Paul, are coming, too. Anyone who comes to town sooner or later makes their way into the best pizza joint around. We need eyes."

"Monty won't quit. I had a restraining order against him while on the case because he approached me a couple times and threatened me."

"And you're just telling me this now?"

"We've been a little busy."

"True." He smiled. "Lots to discuss. Now come on. Let's go meet and talk about how we're going to handle this situation."

Aimi's nervous chuckle died in her mouth as reality sank in. And fear, which must have shown on her face because Jackson put his arm around her.

"Monty won't hurt you or anyone. You have my word on that."

His intense gaze almost made her believe him, but he couldn't guarantee that. Not at all. In fact, to help her put him at risk. Her friends, too. And that scared Aimi more than anything.

CHAPTER ELEVEN

Jackson worked hard to keep from showing his worry. He wasn't sure how it had happened, but Aimi was important to him and the fact that she was in danger shook him down to his boots. Her tears had soaked his shirt and touched his heart. Had the woman never cried before? God, if anything happened to her—

With his alert sheriff's eyes, he kept an eye out for the silver SUV he'd seen earlier. He chose not to tell a nervous Aimi about the vehicle but put a protective arm around her as he helped her into his cruiser. He planned to tell the State Police and the Sheriff's Department about that car so they could keep an eye out.

"I should take my car."

"Humor me. I'd rather you didn't drive anywhere alone right now. We can come get your car later."

Aimi flipped her hair, a sign of irritation he already understood, but she got in the cruiser. Jackson sent a thank you skyward and walked around the car.

Everyone was at the Sheriff's Office when they arrived. Dana rushed up to Aimi and hugged her, bringing fresh tears to Aimi's eyes.

"Don't you ever scare me like that again," she told Aimi, all fight gone out of her voice.

"I didn't want you involved. Hell, I still don't. There's no telling what this guy might do and I don't trust him to keep things between him and me. I saw some of the underhanded tactics he tried to learn Helen's whereabouts."

Dana looked around. "Well, we've got more heads than he does and we'll figure this out."

Paul, Bernie's husband, reached over to pat Aimi's hand. "You're not doing this alone."

Jackson had formulated a strategy on the way there. Now, all he had to do was convince Aimi it was the best way to protect her.

"So what's the plan?" Josh asked.

"First, we need to find the man. His name is Monty Smoots. Everyone needs to keep their eyes open for a silver Lexus SUV. I didn't get the license, but I'm sure that's what this guy is driving. I saw a car down the street from Aimi's, with someone in it. When I approached, he took off."

"And you didn't tell me?" Aimi said.

"You had enough on your mind."

Aimi rose from her seat next to Dana and planted her five-foot-three self in front of Jackson's six-foot-three frame. "Let's get this straight. You do not keep those kinds of secrets from me. Sure, I had a little crying jag back at the office. I'm as guilty as anyone of feeling sorry for myself once in a while. But I am not, I repeat, I am not bone china. I have backbone and strength and this is my situation. You need to tell me when you see or learn something related to it." She poked him in the chest. "Got it?"

God, he loved the fire in her eyes. He hoped he'd never have to be on the opposite side of Aimi Larson in court. Wow. He'd never get away with anything around this woman and he didn't mind a bit. Sparring with her was probably as much fun as sex would be. Almost. But if his imagination was even close to the truth, sex would win out.

"Got it," he answered, holding back the salute but unable to stop the grin. She narrowed her eyes.

"You're right, okay?" Jackson said. He wound a lock of her hair around his finger and lowered his voice. "You are precious to me and I'm in total protection mode, but I shouldn't keep you out of the loop. I won't make that mistake again."

"See that you don't." With a quick nod, she backed up and sat down again.

Jackson looked around at the grinning faces and rolled his eyes. He'd probably never live this down. Josh slapped him on the back. "You're in deep, my friend."

So deep. For now, he needed to get things back on track. "I'm going to run his record. If there's anything we can arrest him for, I will do exactly that."

"And if there isn't?"

"Then I think we need to have a man-to-man conversation with Mr. Monty Smoots. When we slap him with the restraining order."

"Little good the one I got in Spokane did me. Apparently, they're nothing but pieces of paper to him."

"Aimi, you should come stay with us," Dana said.

"No." Jackson didn't mean to use his authority voice, but everyone stopped and looked at him.

"What I mean is, I think the best person to help Aimi keep an eye out for this guy is me." He turned to Aimi and reached for her hand, glad when she didn't pull it away. "Stay with me until we sort this out."

"Where, on top of the jail?" Josh asked.

"I bought a house."

"What?" Josh said. "You never said a word."

"I don't generally talk about my private life. But yes, I have a house. Moved in about a month ago." He turned back to Aimi. "There's plenty of room and I can protect you better there."

"I—I don't know."

"Or I'll come stay with you at the shop. I don't care where. I just care that you're safe."

"What about your job?"

"I'll get my shifts covered. And if I have to take a call, you can hang with Josh and Dana."

"Or with us," Bernie and Paul said in unison.

Aimi chewed her lower lip, but she wasn't flicking her hair. That was a good sign. Jackson waited impatiently, but he waited, knowing she needed time to make the choice herself. That she would balk at losing control.

"I would prefer to deal with this myself and not pull you all into my problems," she finally said. "I'm worried one of you will get hurt."

Everyone opened their mouths to respond, but Aimi held up a hand. "But I recognize that this has gone beyond my ability to handle. I'm very grateful for all your help, especially you, Jackson."

When Aimi reached for his hand, Jackson wanted to pump his fist in gratitude. He saw Dana's raised eyebrows and couldn't quite wipe the grin off his face.

"I'll take you up on that offer to stay at your place," Aimi said. "I don't think I'd sleep a wink otherwise."

Jackson nodded, finding it hard to talk. That she could trust him when she hadn't known him very long and after what she'd been through. He treasured that trust. "I won't let you down."

"It's not a matter of you letting me down. It's a matter of Monty's insistence that I pay his price. He's not going to like this, and I'm worried about retaliation. Against all of you."

Paul put an arm around his pregnant wife's shoulder. "We'll keep a sharp eye out."

"We will, too," Dana said.

"Dana, he may know you," Aimi said. She started chewing that lower lip again.

"She won't be alone," Josh said. "I can work from anywhere, so I'll be at Tangerine Treasures when she's there."

"And I'm working from the pizza parlor already," Paul said. "So far, trying to talk the mayor out of his office hasn't worked."

"Hey, I need that office," Josh said.

"You have an office in your accounting firm and at your home. Why do you need a third?" Paul asked.

"It makes me look official."

Everyone laughed at that. Josh Morgan had done a great job as mayor of Willow Bay, but he was the least official-looking person in town. The laughter broke up the somber mood.

"I guess that means we have a plan," Jackson said.

Aimi stood and suggested they go get her car.

"Let's leave your car where it is. Try to confuse the guy a bit."

"I need my car."

"Need?"

"Okay, I want my car. I need that little bit of proof that I have some independence, whether I do or not at the moment. And, I want my own way out in case Smoots gets too close. For my own piece of mind."

Jackson looked out the window for a moment, thinking. "I tell you what. Let's go check out my house, then we'll go get your car. I'd like to put a little distance between us and your office for a while."

With a flick of her hair, Aimi begrudgingly agreed. They all said their goodbyes and promised to stay close in touch. Dana hugged Aimi. "Don't scare me like that again, okay?"

"I won't. I promise."

Once Jackson had Aimi ensconced in his cruiser, he took a moment to look around. No silver SUV, no one standing around that he could see, and he had sharp eyes. He got in the car, vowing that he would keep Aimi safe no matter what.

She was all that mattered. Nothing else.

~~~

Surprised when they drove out of Willow Bay, Aimi found her curiosity mounting despite the drama in her life. What kind of house would Jackson buy? Ranch or two-story? Craftsman or something with modern edges? She tended toward modern, but she'd bet anything Jackson was a Craftsman kind of man.

When they pulled up to the two-story house, she felt vindicated. "A Craftsman-style home, huh?"

"On the outside." He grinned, then got out and went around the car, checking the street both ways before he opened her door.

That brought the world crashing back in around Aimi. He was her protection. Surprised that she found comfort in that, his concern for her safety also grated against her need to set her own course in life. She could take care of herself. Or so she'd thought, right up until recent events. Aimi was smart enough to know when she needed help, and she needed it now. The real question was whether or not she wanted to see where this thing with Jackson could go. They probably couldn't even begin to sort that out until this business with Monty was finished. If it ever got finished.
~~~

Inside the house, Aimi's mouth opened in surprise to see the difference from the traditional façade outside. She could see straight through to the kitchen. Everything was wide open and light. White quartz countertops, white upper cabinets, navy blue lowers.

The living room, instead of being overfull with leather wrap-around furniture, was empty save for a recliner and end table. And the requisite guy television, probably sixty-plus inches.

"Umm, I haven't had time to buy furniture."

"I can see that. But the place looks great. It's a lot more modern than I thought it would be."

"I have some things I want to renovate. Both the bathrooms are on the old side, so I've talked to Luke, our local carpenter, about remodeling." He led the way down the hall and into what had to be the master. The king-size bed was huge but didn't look it in the spacious room, even if it was the only piece of furniture. A turned-over wooden crate managed as a bedside table.

"It's... well, it's big," Aimi said.

"The bed? Yes. I wanted plenty of room." He grinned at her and Aimi grew warm thinking about where his imagination was going.

"Anyhow, you can sleep in here."

"Where will you sleep?"

"With you."

The silence between them grew like a balloon being filled until it was close to bursting. "I'm not sure I'm ready for that."

"And if you're not, there's a blow-up mattress in the closet that, while not quite sized right for my long legs, will do in a pinch."

"I could sleep on the airbed."

"Absolutely not."

Aimi decided to let that sit for a while. "You really could use more furniture."

"One of these days I'll get around to it."

She walked back out to the main room. Her furniture, like her sink-into tan couch and leather arm-chairs, would look great in here. As a matter of fact, so would her bronze and glass end tables.

"Hey, I've got an idea," she said. "All my furniture is in storage. Why don't we go get some of it for this place? Just the couch, maybe. At least that way, while I'm here, we'll be comfortable."

"Do you have a bed?"

Jackson's deflated look made her laugh. "I donated my bed. It was old and I knew I'd want to buy new when I got settled. So no bed. Sorry."

"I'm not." His eyes gleamed.

"But I've also got some stool that would fit at your kitchen island."

"Want to move in?"

Aimi froze and Jackson did, too. Apparently, he hadn't meant to say that. But he didn't shy away from it. He pulled her into his arms and kissed her. "I get that it's too soon for that. I was running with the moment. I don't know where this is going, Aimi, but I want to explore it. I'm more attracted to you than I've ever been to anyone. I think of you when I'm with you and when I'm not. I want to see where we can go."

With her hands resting on his chest, she sorted through her thoughts and emotions. His heart kept up a steady tha-thump as he waited. Her gut told her to trust him, and she definitely wanted to know him in every sense. But was she ready?

"I'm not sure I'm ready for this," she said.

Jackson started to back off, but Aimi grabbed him around the waist and pulled him in tight. "I'm not sure I'm ready," she started again, "but I think about you, too. And I'd like to explore… us, too. Maybe we can take it slow and easy?"

Jackson's grin lit up the already light and airy room. "Any way you like it. You call the shots, ma'am."

He dipped his head, capturing Aimi's lips in a soft, sweet, promise of what would come. Aimi leaned into him, accepting his promise. Hip to hip, heart to heart, she opened herself up to the possibilities of them. Her body responded as deeply as her heart. Aimi wiggled against Jackson, feeling his arousal.

He broke the kiss and set her back. "If we keep this up, we'll be in that bed together before you're ready."

"I think I'm ready now."

"I want you to know for sure. No question. For now, let's do what you asked. Slow and easy, okay?"

Damn. The man was right, but her raging hormones didn't want to agree. Still, Aimi reached up and pecked him on the cheek. "Thanks for being the strong one. I'm going to use the ladies' room."

"Yeah," she heard him mutter as she walked away. "Real smart idea, Jackson. Take things slow."

A huge grin lit Aimi's face as she walked out of the room. Huge.

CHAPTER TWELVE

Aimi woke up after the best night's sleep she'd had in a long time. It was quiet at Jackson's house. Well, mostly quiet. She'd listened to the air mattress whoosh and groan as Jackson tossed and turned. He probably didn't sleep all that well. Tonight, she'd make sure he took the bed. Hell, maybe it was time for them to both sleep in the bed. She'd almost broken down and invited him last night. She'd taken a while to get to sleep, thinking about what they could be doing in this big bed.

Today was a brand-new day and, for the first time in a long time, Aimi was filled with hope. She stretched and glanced at her phone.

Don't think that sheriff will stop me. You ruined my life and you will pay for that.

Her situation crashed back into her like a rogue wave. Oh, God. Did he know where she was? He would not leave this alone. Aimi felt, deep in her soul, that things were escalating. More people were being drawn into Monty's web. He wouldn't leave them be without making certain they understood that he would have his revenge.

"Good morning," Jackson said, leaning against the door frame. His smile disappeared when he saw her. He was at the bed in an instant, taking her phone from her hands. He scowled as he read the message, and his body tensed. Even so, he reached for her hand and held it with such gentleness that Aimi started to cry. How could two men be so different? One dangerously, selfishly obsessed, one thinking more about her than himself.

Letting instinct guide her, Aimi pulled her phone out of Jackson's hands and set it on the nightstand. When he looked at her, the wild rage in his eyes softened. Aimi cupped his face and pulled him closer.

"I'm a little worried I'm falling for you, Sheriff Smith."

Any echo of rage disappeared. "Only a little worried?"

She shrugged. "Maybe a lot worried. But right now, I don't want to worry." She closed the distance between them, watching Jackson's eyes widen as their lips touched. He caught on quickly and wrapped his arms around her, deepening the kiss, running his hands up through her sleep-mussed hair, along her neck and shoulders. Her lips opened on a sigh and he took advantage. He tasted like really great coffee. Aimi let herself go, exploring him with her lips and hands, learning the back, the arms, the jaw of the man she was about to invite into bed.

Jackson pulled away, a clear question on his face even as his eyes shone with intensity.

"Yes," Aimi whispered.

He leaped up and over her, landing in the middle of the bed, then pulled her to him, laughing. Laughter that died immediately when she cupped him through his sweats.

"Woman," he gasped. "Give a man some warning."

"Why? Are you going to say no?" She grinned, loving the power she held.

That power lasted all of three seconds. The mischief in his eyes warned her, just barely, before he grabbed both of her hands and held them over her head.

"So we're playing it like that, are we?" he said. "Fair warning. I give as good as I get."

He lowered his head to her neck to gently suck her skin, kissing along the neckline of the t-shirt she'd slept in.

Aimi shuddered under the onslaught of his lips and tongue. When he pulled her nipple into his mouth, shirt and all, she arched off the bed.

"Holy shit," she murmured as his touch radiated to her core, setting her on fire.

Jackson raised his head, his eyes gleaming. "Told you. Now, let's get this shirt off."

"And those sweats."

"Works for me," he said, releasing her hands.

After she yanked her shirt off, Aimi watched him stand and shed his pants. Those muscles of his weren't limited to his arms and torso. His well-defined legs showcased a gorgeously erect penis that Aimi reached for without thought. Oh, did she want to play with this bad boy.

"Uh uh," Jackson said, climbing back on the bed. "It's my turn."

In one fluid move, he captured her hands above her head again. Aimi didn't argue. Body and soul, she tingled with the need to be touched by Jackson. She wanted all of him, wanted to give him everything she had. He kissed his way back to her breasts and Aimi sighed with pleasure. Licking, nipping, caressing—his talented tongue raised her desire to a level beyond her experience. When he released her arms with a quiet "stay" she wrapped her fingers around the wood slats of his headboard, more than willing to comply.

He trailed kisses along her belly, spread her legs and settled there, his hot breath fanning her core. That's all it took for her to just about come off the bed.

"You like?" he asked.

"Oh, yes. I like."

Before she could utter another word, he covered her with his mouth, his tongue delving into the deepest parts of her.

Too much.

Too fast.

Jackson touched her soul and she flew, shaking with her release for so long she barely noticed he hadn't stopped. Instead, he renewed his efforts, taking her back to the edge.

"Break. I need... break."

"One more time, sweetheart. Just one more," he murmured, teasing her mercilessly with his tongue.

Her hips rose without choice and she soared over the edge again. Up, up, up, on one gigantic spasm that rolled on and on and on until she was boneless and floating in a haze of sensuality.

Time stopped as she lay there, spent and happier than she could ever remember being. The bed rocked and rolled as Jackson moved back beside her, holding out a condom package. "Care to do the honors?"

"I'm not sure I can even move," she answered, but reached for the foil pack, and for Jackson. She poured everything into kissing him. Every still-raging nerve ending, every emotion, every thought. All for him.

Aimi sat up and pushed him gently back onto the bed, running her hands all over him. Starting with his short hair, knuckling softly along his cheek. She leaned down and kissed his neck in just that spot where he'd mesmerized her. She followed the bone of his clavicle to the center of his chest, running her hands through the curly hair.

Straddling him, she smiled when his cock jumped against her.

"Impatient, aren't we?" she said, smiling.

"Yes," he growled. "Sheath me or I'll take care of it."

"Don't think so," she said. "You're not the only one with abilities here, though yours are... Well, there are no words to describe where you took me, but now, it's my turn."

She took her time, feathering her hands over his nipples, then her lips. He shuddered with need, making her heady with power. She scooted down so she could wander her way along his stomach, following the line of hair that ended at a very proud, very stiff cock. Then, she did to him what he did to her, though not for long. He pulled her mouth away.

"You vixen. I won't make it much longer."

The intensity in his gaze proved his statement, so Aimi ripped open the foil packet with her mouth and, with utter care and slowness, slid the condom down his length.

"Aimi," he ground out.

In answer, she shifted forward and slid onto him, taking his impressive girth in one fell swoop.

He groaned, his hands moving to her hips. "God, you feel good."

"So do you," she whispered, feeling the need grow again. She slid almost off, then back down. Slow. Slower.

Until Jackson flipped her over on her back without separating them. He kissed her, long and hard, then moved inside her. Fast, faster, faster still. Pounding her, taking her back to the edge and over just as his own release hit.

Breathing hard, they lay there for who knew how long, reveling in the feel of each other and their climaxes. Slowly coming down from the heights and back to normal space.

~~~

Jackson's arms shook from the effort of being on top of her, but not weighing her down. He rolled to the side and
~~~

pulled her with him. Replete. Complete. Nothing had ever felt like that before. He'd seen fucking stars as he'd come. Stars!

"Holy shit," Aimi said, throwing an arm over her eyes.

"Yeah. Holy shit. Isn't that where we started?" He still couldn't breathe normally and wasn't sure when he'd be able to again. One thing Jackson did know. He'd stay in bed with her forever if he could.

"That was... spectacular," Aimi said.

"Beyond."

"Yeah."

Daylight filtered in through the windows. Jackson glanced at the bedside clock. "You're late opening your office."

"Who cares."

"Agreed."

"Besides, we're going to my storage facility to get some furniture, right?"

"Sure. If you still want to."

"I want places to sit while I'm here. I can't stay in this bed all day."

"I'd be happy if we did."

Aimi laughed and kissed him. "I bet you would. Shower time for me, though." She got up and sashayed her ass across to his bathroom door. Just before disappearing, she glanced at him over her shoulder with a sly smile. "Going to come wash my back?"

Oh, hell yes. Jackson leaped out of bed like a puppy being offered a treat. He grabbed another condom packet and headed for the shower. He'd wash her back, her front, her everything.

<center>~~~</center>

Two hours later, they stood in front of Aimi's storage unit.

"You have a lot of sh— stuff," Jackson said, eyeing the stacked-to-the-ceiling locker.

"Not that much," Aimi said, happy to see her furniture again.

"This is the largest locker they rent here."

"Hey," she said, giving Jackson a fist-tap on his shoulder. "I worked hard for this."

"There's no way this all came from your condo. I don't even think this would fit in my house." He was full-on laughing by now.

"Okay, you're teasing me. It would totally fit, and it was perfect in the condo."

From behind, he encircled her with his arms and pulled her against his chest. "I'm not so sure," he said, still chuckling. "I know one thing, though. I didn't bring a big enough truck."

Aimi whirled, giving him a mock glare. "That'll be quite enough out of you, mister. If you want the use of my furniture, you'd better stop teasing me."

"Hey, this was your idea."

"And I'm about to renege on the offer, even as nice as I am. Look. The furniture's in the front. Easy to get to without having to disturb everything."

"Then I guess I should be thankful for small miracles."

"You should. Now come on. Let's wrestle what you want into your truck and get them back to your place."

"You sure you can help me lift all this?"

This time, the glare Aimi leveled at Jackson wasn't at all faked.

He held up his hands. "All right, all right. Let's get it done."

The couch and bar stools fit, but barely. Aimi and Jackson stood on opposite sides of the bed, tossing a rope back and forth to secure the load.

Pop! Pop! Pop!

Were those gunshots?

"Down, Aimi!" Jackson yelled, ducking himself. "Get down. Stay down."

Aimi dove for the ground, her heart hammering, thinking she could crawl under the truck. Turns out, all those shows where people hid under vehicles sure made it look easier than it was. Jackson, on the ground on his side, peered at Aimi while he radioed for help.

"Stay down, Aimi." His voice, while filled with urgency, held that admirable calmness she'd grown to expect from him. "Based on where I think the bullets came from, he can't get to us here on the ground." He paused as his radio squawked. "Help is on the way." He reached for her from his side of the truck. "Just breathe. Stay calm."

She grabbed his hand and held on tight. Between the visceral feel of her hand in his and the way he maintained their eye contact, she started to breathe normally instead of drawing in great gulps of air.

"Good," Jackson said. "Just like that."

A siren sounded in the distance, getting closer.

"They're coming fast."

"Yep. They'll be here in moments and they'll secure the area so we can get you to a safer place."

"I'm staying with you."

"Not until we either catch this guy or know for certain he's gone."

"Jackson— "

"No argument permitted. This is my job and I'm going to keep you safe. Understand?"

Oh, Aimi understood all right. She just didn't like it much, damn it. What was happening to her? Even though she didn't like him giving her orders, she didn't have much choice right then. She was shaking, badly, and couldn't think straight. Still…

"I can't do my job if I know you're in danger, Aimi. Please."

And didn't that just deflate her righteous anger? Damn it all. He'd said please. "Fine," she ground out, still miffed, but recognizing he was right.

"Thank you."

"Just don't get used to me following orders."

"Why would I ever get used to that?" Jackson flashed his wicked smile her way, a smile that calmed her, made her feel safe, as a sheriff's cruiser roared into the yard and parked in front of the truck.

"Stay here until I check-in. Then we'll move you to the office."

When he let go of her hand, Aimi's panic threatened to return. However, in only moments he was helping her up. "Crouch low," he said, and shielded her until they reached the storage facility's office door. Jackson checked inside, where Pete, the owner, had taken refuge behind his counter. He came up holding a rifle.

"Keep her safe, Pete, while we check out the area."

"Will do."

Aimi grabbed Jackson's arm. "Be careful."

Again he flashed that smile, then, with a tug on her ponytail, he was gone. Several minutes passed. Minutes that seemed more like hours. Aimi paced back and forth no matter how much Pete tried to get her to come behind the counter with him.

Finally, the door opened and Jackson stepped back inside.

"Are you all right?" Aimi flew to his side.

Jackson held out his arms and twirled in a circle. "No injuries here."

"Did you catch him?" She let the hope seep out for a second or two until Jackson shook his head.

"We found the spot he shot from, but he was gone."

"Damn." Aimi walked to the window and glanced up and down the street. She'd about had it with this guy. She'd come to Willow Bay to start over, not to be harassed by some psycho. Aimi welcomed her anger. It beat the hell out of being afraid.

"We'll find him," Jackson said, coming up behind her.

She whirled around. "Oh, you bet your sweet ass we'll find him. I've about had it with this guy disrupting my life."

"I do have one more bit of bad news," Jackson said. Given the look on his face, Aimi knew she wasn't going to like what he had to say.

"Out with it."

"Two of the bullets went through your ivory leather couch."

"What? I want to see."

Beside the truck, Aimi stuck her hand through a small hole in her prize leather sectional. Oh, yeah. They were definitely going to catch this guy and when they did, she wanted the first crack at him.

She was done being Miss Nice Guy. The gloves were off.

CHAPTER THIRTEEN

Jackson spent two days trying to distract Aimi and cool her anger and frustration. Every local law enforcement entity was searching for Monty Smoots, but the guy had disappeared. There'd been no clues to his whereabouts and extra patrols were running 24/7.

He was pretty frustrated himself, so he understood where Aimi was at. The only thing keeping either of them sane was being together. He couldn't get enough of her. Not just in bed, though sex with Aimi was the best he'd ever had. He genuinely enjoyed being around her, cooking with her, talking to her, listening to her, except maybe for the recurring discussion they were having right now.

"I still think our hiding isn't going to help find this guy," Aimi said for about the fifth time that day as they unloaded the dishwasher together. "We need to be out there. Force him to make a mistake and show himself."

"And that puts you square in the sights of his rifle. No thank you," Jackson said, running a hand over his unruly hair. He needed a haircut, but not until they found Monty Smoots. His heart had about stopped when he realized the man had fired at Aimi. He couldn't let that happen again. He wouldn't, no matter what she said.

"What are you going to do if I want to go out? Handcuff me to the bed to keep me here?"

The thought thoroughly distracted him. Even Aimi paused, blushing to her gorgeous, naturally dark roots. Jackson smiled.

"You know damn well what I meant," she said.

"I do, but I still went there, and so did you." He grinned. Couldn't help himself.

"Yes, well, get your mind out of the gutter and explain again how sitting here holed up in your house is helping to capture Monty."

His phone rang, saving him from having to answer.

~~~

Aimi watched the laughter fade from Jackson's face as he listened, replaced by a scowl. "I want in."

"Fine. Be there in half an hour." Jackson hung up the phone and turned to her.

Conflict was written all over his face.

"You've got a call you need to take?"

As much as Aimi wanted to bring Monty down and get back to normal life, she'd grown used to having Jackson around. They'd spent most of the last couple days tracking down leads from his house, calling around town, to no avail. They worked together well, though. They played off one another, throwing thoughts back and forth. Their ideas and deductions were great, but still, they had no leads.

It wasn't just that. Jackson made her feel at home. Safe. Comfortable. Her couch, bullet hole and all, looked good in his house. But that wasn't why she'd settled in so easily. Aimi hadn't planned to fall for anyone anytime soon, and certainly not one as stubborn or domineering as Jackson could be. That promise to herself had flown out the door.
~~~

"A call?" he said. "Yes and no. There's a tip."

"About time. Let me get my jacket."

"Uh, no."

"What do you mean, no?"

"It's too dangerous. You can't go."

"The hell I can't."

"Aimi—"

"Look, Smoots has completely disrupted my life. I have a right to be involved in his capture."

Jackson pulled her into his arms. "You do. But you can't."

"You can't tell me what to do."

"In this case, I can. This is a law enforcement response and it could very easily get ugly. You cannot be there. I need to know you're safe. I'll drop you at Josh and Dana's."

Aimi backed away to make sure he saw the resolve in her face. She did not need to be coddled. "I'm not going to Dana's house."

"Yes, you are."

She shook her head. "I'm not."

"I'm not leaving you home alone."

"Your house is damn near a fortress with the alarm system you installed. I'll be fine here."

"Not happening." By the set of his mouth, Aimi already knew she would lose this battle. But damn, she hated it when he went all caveman on her.

"Just so you know, this is exactly the guy trait I've tried so hard to escape." As soon as she said it, she clapped a hand over her mouth. "I'm so sorry, Jackson. I'm not comparing you to the bully in Spokane. It's a natural inclination of mine to pull out all the stops when someone gives me an order."

The thin line of his mouth eased. "And you'd better be damn glad I know that about you already, or I'd have taken that personally. Now, grab what you need. We leave in five."

She'd lost the argument all on her own. Damn it. Dutifully, she was back downstairs in five minutes with her bag. "Just don't think you ordering me around is going to be the norm, mister."

Jackson laughed. "Life with you, Aimi Larson, will never be predictable or boring." He held out his arm.

"I hope not," she said, and as she slipped her arm through his, she knew she wanted the chance to prove that statement over a long, long time.

At Josh and Dana's house, Jackson escorted her inside and thanked them for stepping up to help.

"No problem," Josh said. "I was already working from home."

After a smoldering kiss that promised much more later, Aimi watched Jackson head out. He needed to do his job. Once the door closed behind him, she sank down on the couch. Dana sat next to her as Josh handed glasses of iced tea around.

"Do many of the calls Jackson gets turn dangerous or violent?" Aimi asked Josh.

"Not too many. We're a peace-loving community for the most part. The occasional domestic dispute can go south. And there's always the chance of a drug deal gone wrong. Mostly, though, it's theft and shoplifting."

"And the occasional beach rescue," Aimi said.

Josh grinned. "Yes. That, too."

"Damn it. I don't want someone in my life that I have to worry about."

"Like he worries about you?" Josh said.

"Too late," Dana piped in.

"You two are no help at all, you know that?"

"That's because we think you and Jackson are perfect for each other."

Aimi rolled her eyes. "I'm going to have to find another friend if I want to have a real discussion about this."

Dana's bad job of looking appalled made Aimi laugh. After that, the three of them chatted about life in Willow Bay for a while, then Josh said he was going upstairs to get some more work done.

"You definitely got a good one there, Dana."

"I did." She watched him head up the steps with a soft glow in her eyes and the hint of a smile. "I love him so much." She turned to Aimi. "And it feels so good, I want that for you."

"I want it, too. But with Jackson? I'm just not sure about him. About us."

"What's not to be sure of? He's steady, gorgeous, and dotes on you."

"He's also pig-headed and barks orders like a drill sergeant sometimes."

"Hmmm. Sounds like someone else I know."

"Me? I'm completely offended by that." Aimi tried to keep the stern look on her face, but it didn't last. She dissolved into a fit of laughter, Dana following closely behind.

"Ah, you're good for my soul, Dana."

"Ditto, my friend." Dana hugged her. "Now, you said you brought some work with you?"

"Yes, ummm, just finishing up flyers for the new business. Speaking of work, it's Wednesday. Why aren't you at the shop?"

"I wasn't feeling too great this morning. I've hired an assistant. Mary Crocker's daughter, and she agreed to run the shop today. She starts community college next month and needed a job. We'll have to work around her school hours, but I won't be so tied to the store. I do have my own set of tasks to get through, though. Josh is a real stickler for keeping the books up to date."

"I'd expect he would be, being an accountant." Aimi stood with her bag and briefcase. Jackson was working. It was time for her to do the same. "Okay if I set up at the dining room table?"

"That's great. I think I'm going to lay right here and take a nap."

"You do look a little pale."

"Probably just the morning sickness." Dana rubbed her stomach. "Juniorette is making my life a bit hellish at the moment."

"Can I do anything to help?"

"Josh takes wonderful care of me on my down days, and doesn't complain one bit."

"He's definitely a keeper."

"Oh, yes, he certainly is."

"Well, dinner's on me tonight. You are not lifting a finger."

"I like that idea." Dana scrunched a pillow and laid down, letting Aimi cover her with the afghan.

"It's cool in here. You don't want to get chilled."

"Thank you." Dana gripped Aimi's hand for a moment, then closed her eyes.

At the table, Aimi watched Dana's breathing ease as she fell asleep. She was worried about her friend. She'd have to ask Josh if Dana and the baby really were all right.

Saying a quick prayer that they were, Aimi opened her briefcase. Contrary to what she told Dana about working on flyers, she pulled out all the information she and Jackson had pulled together about Monty and spread the paperwork out on the table. Jackson may have a tip on where the guy was holed up, but Aimi had back up plans. Information was key to finding this guy and that was her forte.

Monty Smoots' criminal record wasn't clean, but it wasn't horrible. Traffic infractions and one bar fight that landed him in jail. Helen had called in spousal abuse twice, but had refused to charge him. Aimi shook her head. It took a lot of hard work to help abused spouses understand the abuse is not their fault and there are people out there who want to help. No one needs to stay in that situation.

Monty didn't have a job that she could determine. In fact, the only funds he had came from social security. He was what, forty-five? Helen said she'd been attracted to the fact that he was a little older than she was. That was supposed to mean he was beyond all the macho shit younger men exhibited, or so her client had thought.

Except he hadn't been. Thank goodness Helen was safely away.

She fingered the paper showing his bank account before his divorce from Helen. How did someone get social security at his age? There really was only one way. Disability. Yet, back then, he'd had a job at the local sports store.

Aimi pushed the papers aside. Nothing made sense, except that Monty Smoots needed serious help. Aimi would not be the one to get him that. She just wanted him out of her life.

Her phone beeped.

Hey, beautiful. Sorry about the orders earlier. I know that's not your thing and I appreciate that you went along with it.

Jackson. She smiled. Just thinking about him made her warm all over.

I haven't stopped thinking of you since you left.

Me, either.

Is the tip credible?

Not sure yet.

Aimi wanted to ask more, but if she didn't give Jackson time to do his job, what kind of partner would she be. So she kept it simple.

Get back soon.

She wanted to add something more. Maybe Xs and Os? Aimi wasn't an X's and O's kind of person, though, so she sent the message as is.

I hope to.

She held the phone to her chest, wishing it was Jackson and not an inanimate object. Would she always worry about him like this? Her life was changing at a whirlwind pace and she hadn't thought everything through. Jackson had woven his way into her heart with patience and kindness. And hotness. Lots of hotness. A kiss alone could send her reeling into a sensual space she'd never known before. Was this love? Aimi, who applied logic to almost everything she did, tried to analyze their relationship, but it defied description. When they'd first met, the physical attraction went way beyond the one-to-ten scale. He'd given her time. Not much, but some. And now, she missed him in every way. She loved talking to him, being quiet with him, being in bed with him. The times they'd worked together proved they could focus and still enjoy each other. And, more than anyone in her life, Jackson made her feel safe. It surprised her that she liked that cocoon around her, even if it meant the occasional toe-to-toe discussions and order-barking. Yet, even with his overbearing personality, Jackson listened to her wants, her needs, and as much as possible, put them ahead of his own.

She suspected she was more selfish than him, but she tried to give back, to repay him for the way he made her feel. Safe. Cherished. Loved.

And she loved him. She knew that now. Moving to Willow Bay had brought nothing but surprises. Aimi was ready to embrace them, and Jackson. She could hardly wait until he got back so they could talk about all this. In the meantime, she picked up the bank statement again and stared at it. Monty needed to be dealt with before she and Jackson could truly explore this thing between them.

A while later, she looked at her phone. Jackson had thought he'd be an hour or two. No more. Three hours had passed, and he hadn't contacted her to say he'd be delayed. She'd never been the clingy type, but her nerves were about shot, so she texted him.

You almost done?

Aimi waited ten minutes, then texted him again.

Sorry. Busy. Tell you when I get home. You good?

I'm fine. Do what you need to do.

Dana moaned from the front room and Aimi went to check on her. Tangled in the blankets, Dana had a hand over her mouth and tried to get the blanket off with the other.

"Sick," she mumbled.

After detangling Dana from the blanket, Aimi rushed with her to the bathroom.

"Josh," she hollered up the stairs as they passed.

In seconds, he pounded down the stairs and into the bathroom to hold his wife's hair back.

"Wet a washcloth, Aimi."

She did, and handed it to him. "She doesn't look good."

"She's lost weight, and this keeps happening all day long. She isn't keeping anything down."

"Right here," Dana mumbled.

"And I think you should be in the hospital," Josh said.

"Me, too."

"No," Dana said, then retched again for several long moments. "Okay, maybe."

"Done."

"Want me to call 9-1-1?" Aimi asked.

"Not going in an ambulance," Dana croaked out.

"I'll drive her," Josh said. "Stay with her while I get her purse and our phones."

Five minutes later, they had Dana bundled in the passenger seat.

His face awash in misery, Josh looked at Aimi. "I doubt they'll let you come into the ER with us."

"I'll be fine."

"I promised Jackson we'd keep you safe."

"I am safe. Look, I'm going to clean up inside, then lock up. I'll take Dana's car straight to Jackson's house. His alarm system is top-notch."

"Jackson will kill me."

"He's not here. I am. And I'll text him that it was my choice. Now go. Take care of Dana. I'll text you when I'm safe inside Jackson's house."

He looked at her, a war of indecision on his face until Dana moaned.

"Go!" Aimi said.

He got in the car and flew off down the road.

Alone for the first time in days, Aimi hugged herself, shivering even in the summer heat. She looked all around. Nothing seemed out of place. Back in the house, she locked the door and cleaned up the bathroom, then loaded her briefcase up. Unwilling to worry Jackson, she'd wait until she was safe inside his house before texting him. Within minutes, she was in Dana's car and on her way to Jackson's, keeping a sharp eye out for Monty's silver Lexus SUV. She even drove around the block before parking and going in.

At the door, she noticed the alarm wasn't on. Why wasn't it? Jackson was fastidious about arming the thing. Aimi stared at it for a long moment, trying to quell the uneasiness churning in her stomach. Jackson must have been so focused on getting her to Josh and Dana's that he forgot to set it up. She nodded her head as she tried to convince herself of that because it just didn't sound like Jackson.

She locked the door and armed the system, then picked up a fireplace poker and painstakingly searched the house, finding it empty. Aimi took her first really deep breath in a while. She was safe. And more tired than she'd been in a long time. She texted Jackson, then Josh to say she was inside the house and found out Josh and Dana had arrived at the hospital and were waiting on some lab results, but Dana was stable. They'd given her something for the nausea.

With a yawn, Aimi decided to lie down for a nap. She stretched out on the bed, running her hands over Jackson's pillow. A noise made her jump. One of the house's many creaks. Still hugging Jackson's pillow tight, she tried to drift off to sleep with one eye open.

CHAPTER FOURTEEN

Jackson had actually begun to pray that Willow Bay would settle the hell down. The whole town seemed out of sorts. After the bogus tip on Monty's whereabouts, he and Rob had answered calls back-to-back for the last two hours. The first one, a domestic, had de-escalated before he arrived. Good thing, too, because he wasn't focused on the job. He couldn't stop thinking about Aimi. Worrying about her. And the two blockheads in front of him now, about to come to blows over a minor fender-bender, tried his patience like nothing else.

Having checked in with Aimi a little over an hour ago, Jackson knew things were fine. He hadn't been happy that she'd gone home by herself, but she was safe inside and his alarm was top notch. Maybe he should call again, just to be sure. Before he could pull his phone out, his radio squawked, and he answered with an inward groan.

"Sorry, sheriff, but Rob's still at the scene of that accident on the south side of town and we just got a report of a multicar accident at mile post ninety out on Highway 101."

Ninety? That was a ways out of town. "Any injuries?" If there weren't, maybe he could mail them all accident reports.

"Injuries are reported. Paramedics are en route."

Shit. He couldn't let this one handle itself. With a sigh, Jackson said he'd head there straightaway. Sometimes, he hated his job.

After giving the idiots still yelling at each other accident reports to complete and file, along with an empty threat to haul their asses to jail if they didn't calm the hell down, Jackson got on the road.

Twenty minutes later, he caught up to the paramedic unit, who sat on the shoulder of an empty road. Jackson pulled in ahead of them and got out. He walked back to the ambulance.

"Hey, Steve," he greeted the driver. "Where's the accident?"

Steve shrugged. "Don't know. We drove all the way to milepost 88 and saw nothing. Thought we'd hang around until you got here and see if you knew anything more."

"I know as much as you do." Jackson keyed his mike. "Double check on that accident location at milepost ninety, please."

"Report says north of town on the highway, approximately mile post ninety."

"I'm here with the paramedics. They went an extra two miles and saw nothing."

"Supposed to be at least three cars involved in multiple rear-end collisions with injuries."

"Can you verify?"

"I'll give it a try."

While he waited, Jackson sent a text off to Aimi.

All good?

No response came back. Phone in hand, he paced as he waited for her to respond. Damn it, where was she? She had to be at home. She wouldn't go anywhere else, would she? Jackson paced faster as a little voice in his head reminded him of how stubborn she could be. He called her, getting her voicemail.

Jackson's radio squawked again. "Can't verify. Must be a prank call."

Between the bogus call, Dana in the ER, and the fact that Aimi was alone and unprotected, Jackson's gut hit the asphalt. Damn it. Jackson flew to his SUV, a fear he'd never felt before burning through his mind, his heart, every neuron in his body. No way this was a prank. He'd been set up. He called Aimi again. It went to voicemail. Again.

"Aimi, call me as soon as you get this."

He hit the sirens and lights, doing a one-eighty in the road and flying back to town. He reached out to Rob, but the man was farther away than Jackson at a legitimate accident that wasn't cleared yet.

"Shit." Jackson called Aimi again. Still no answer.

"Shit, shit, shit." Jackson took every risk he warned new recruits not to take. He flew past cars, every mile he covered bringing him closer to Aimi. What if's tore through his mind, leaving ragged holes in his heart. Aimi had to be safe. She just had to be. He couldn't lose her. Not now, when he'd just found her and they'd only begun learning about each other. Every instinct he'd ever relied on told him he loved her. Jackson, who'd vowed never to fall in love or marry because that never ended well, had fallen hard and fast for Aimi Larsen. And now she was in danger. He couldn't lose her. God, please, she had to be okay.

He pounded the steering wheel, forced to slow down by oncoming traffic and an RV in front of him. Precious seconds passed before he got around the vacationer.

Back in town, lights and sirens didn't seem to mean much to the meandering folks who'd left their worries behind for a few days. Didn't people know to pull over?

Finally, after what seemed like hours, Jackson screeched to a halt halfway up the grass in front of his house, threw the car into park, leaped out, and raced up the steps.

The sheriff in him automatically cataloged what he saw. No forced entry. Good. The alarm was on, just as Aimi had said. The door was locked and Jackson cursed the time it took to dig out his keys. Inside, he screamed Aimi's name as he shut off the alarm, then he raced through the house. Her purse and phone were on the kitchen island. Aimi wouldn't go anywhere without them unless she'd been forced.

The window above the washer and dryer was wide open. The only window he didn't have alarmed because he'd thought it too high to reach from the outside.

"Aimi!" Jackson raced out the back door in time to see the gate to the alley slam shut. He ran across the yard and threw open the gate, looking both ways.

Nothing. Whoever had gone through the gate had vanished into thin air. Damn it.

Hoping against all odds, Jackson went back in the house and called for her. "Aimi! Where are you?"

No answer. Oh, God, had Monty taken her? A sound worked its way into Jackson's attention. A sort of scuffling. He turned his head, tuning it in. The bedroom. Jackson took the stairs two at a time, but the bedroom was empty.

More scuffling. Coming from the closet. He opened the door and immediately saw the pile of bedding and clothes at the back of the closet shifting, undulating like some slow-moving mud flow. Mumbled curses came from beneath the pile.

He yanked at the pile, tossing covers and shirts this way and that to find a very disheveled Aimi Larsen at the bottom. "Oh, thank God."

"Get these goddamned things off me," Aimi said, a fierce scowl on her face.

Jackson hauled her into his arms, crushing her against him, so eternally grateful that she was here. Alive.

"Yeah, yeah," Aimi's muffled voice came from tight against his chest. "I'm all right."

Her voice barely registered as blood rushed through his ears and his heart thumped wildly. He pressed her closer, overcome with relief and the residual adrenaline that coursed through his body.

"Let go of me," Aimi said.

"Are you really all right?" He set her back, but not far. He touched her hair, ran his hands along her arms. Other than her hair being a complete mess, she looked unhurt.

"Seriously, I'm fine."

"I was scared to death when I realized you were alone." He shook her a little. "Don't do that to me ever again. You stay put when I tell you to stay put."

Fire filled her eyes. "I would have if Dana hadn't been ill enough to need a hospital, and fast. By the way, I came directly home, watched my surroundings carefully, and dashed into a house that was locked up tight. Plus, I searched the entire house and kept the fireplace poker with me." She pointed to the rod iron tool on the floor. "But somehow, Monty got in."

"He was here?"

"I think so. I laid down, but something woke me up. A noise I didn't think was normal. I had about ten seconds to hide." She pointed to the closet. "That pile of clothes and such stinks to high heaven." Aimi sniffed. "And now I stink."

"Well, yeah. That's my dirty laundry."

"Haven't you ever heard of a hamper?"

He stared at her. "Weren't you even scared?"

Her voice grew quiet and she stopped brushing imaginary dirt off her pants. "Yes. Of course I was. I knew it wasn't you. I was dead asleep. Once I woke, I heard movement in the house and the footsteps were different from yours. More hesitant. I reached for my phone but realized I'd left it in the kitchen. So I did the only thing I could think of—I hid. Good plan, because those footsteps came up the stairs and into the bedroom."

"Did you see him? Can you identify that it was Monty?"

Aimi shook her head. "I closed the door to the closet when I slipped in there so I didn't see anything. Who else could it have been but Monty?"

Damn. It would help if she'd seen him if they hoped to put this guy away. Though Jackson would love nothing more than to get a little time with him first.

"I knew I was going to be okay," she said, her voice starting to shake, "when I heard your siren. I think he heard it too because, based on his footfalls, he ran out of here. He knew that siren was headed for this house."

Jackson let out a long breath as the fear ebbed from his body and he finally calmed down. Aimi, though, had started to shake, her entire body shuddering its way into a solid panic attack. Her breathing grew gaspy and she bent over, clutching her stomach.

After helping Aimi sit on the bed, Jackson wrapped a blanket around her, hugging her tight to his body for warmth. He reminded her she was safe.

"I'm here, sweetheart. You're all right. You're safe."

"It just h-h-hit me. That's t-twice he's gotten close enough to hurt me." She clutched Jackson's arm. "Or hurt the people around me. I c-can't seem to stop shaking."

"It's normal to go through this after a scary situation. An adrenaline letdown. Believe me, I'm going through the same thing. Will you be okay here for a minute? I'm getting you a shot of whiskey."

"I'd rather have vodka," Aimi said. Her weak smile encouraged him.

"Sorry, babe, I'm all out of vodka."

She made a face but nodded her head.

Jackson was back in less than a minute with the whisky he kept in the cupboard and a highball glass. He splashed some of the amber liquid into the glass and handed it to her. "Sip this. It'll help."

"Are you t-trying to get me drunk, sheriff?" Her smile grew.

Good. "Yes, and then I'm going to help you take a shower."

"See," she said, looking up at him.

"What?"

"I told you that laundry pile of yours made me stinky."

Jackson's chuckle stayed with them as Aimi climbed into the shower. He quickly stripped and joined her. With tender care he washed her hair, murmuring words he didn't even realize he was saying. Soothing her. Helping her forget the terror. Helping him forget.

CHAPTER FIFTEEN

The next day, Aimi stood in Dana's kitchen cutting up strawberries for a fruit salad. Dana sat across from her looking slightly less peaked and sipping an Ensure.

"This stuff sucks."

"Yes, but you need calories. And you're keeping that down."

"Thanks to the meds they gave me."

Aimi looked at her friend. "I'm so glad you went to the hospital."

"I guess I am, too. They said it isn't abnormal to have this level of nausea in a pregnancy, that it happens and I'll get past it."

"You should still be there. They had you on IV fluids for a reason."

"I couldn't stand it. I hate hospitals more than most. That's why I'm drinking this." She held up the can with a straw in it. "I just... I'd like to be able to enjoy being pregnant with our baby."

"I'm hoping this dinner I'm cooking will taste good enough to bring you back, so you can share your joy with Josh and the rest of us."

"If it stays down."

Aimi nodded. "I was so scared for you last night."

"You were scared for me? How do you think I felt when I found out you'd been threatened again? I can't believe no one told me until I got home this afternoon."

"No way were we going to worry you. Besides, it was all over anyhow." She dumped the rest of the strawberries in the salad.

"I can't believe he was in the house."

"Yes, it feels a little strange there, knowing that. But I'm okay. Jackson's taking good care of me."

"You're my best friend. I have a right to fuss over you and worry about you."

"As I do over you," Aimi said. "So no more crap about me cooking dinner today."

"All right, all right." Dana smiled. "How's the sheriff doing?"

Aimi peeked her head around the corner into the living room, where Jackson was stretched out on the couch. "Still crashed. I don't think he slept at all last night." A warmth suffused Aimi's body as she stared at nothing, remembering. "He held me all night."

"He's a keeper, Aimi."

"You might be right."

"He's worried about you." Dana reached into the bowl and snagged a blueberry. "So, what's holding you back, Aims?"

"I don't know." She washed raspberries. "He's pretty bossy."

Dana laughed. "You're pretty bossy yourself."

"I know. Spokane kind of cured me of giving over power to anyone else."

"You know, Aims, if you let Spokane mess with your head, they win." Dana grabbed a raspberry and ate it. "The partners of that law firm win, that asshole in the bathroom wins, your mother wins. They all win if you lose yourself to how they treated you.”

“You’re right. I know you are. I just need to be cautious for a while.”

“I get it. But don’t let a good thing pass you by just because you’re worried about a power struggle.”

“I’ll try not to.”

“Try not to what?” Jackson said, joining them, putting his arms around Aimi and kissing her neck.

Dana arched an eyebrow in her friend’s direction.

Heat filled Aimi’s cheeks, but she didn’t push him away. It felt too good in his arms.

“What smells so good?” Jackson said.

“Aimi made my favorite casserole. Chicken, rice, celery, green onions, and lots of almond-topped cheese.”

“It smells wonderful. I hope you made a lot. I’m starving.”

Unusually pleased with the compliment, Aimi smiled up at him as he backed away. “There’s hot coffee and Josh should be home soon. We’ll eat then.”

“Sounds good,” Jackson said, pouring himself a cup of coffee and leaning against the counter.

God, he looked good in those tight-fitting blue jeans. His Gray’s County Sheriff t-shirt, loose enough to be comfortable, still managed to be snug enough to make her drool. Aimi damn near wiped her mouth, and that quirky smile of his reminded her of how well he read her thoughts. But he didn’t say anything. Instead, he turned to Dana.

“You’re looking better this afternoon.”

“I’m feeling better,” she said. “And yes,” she said, holding the now empty Ensure can up. “I’m following orders.”

"Good. I don't want to have to arrest you and return you to the hospital," he said, laughing.

"You could try," Dana said so quietly that only Aimi heard her. They shared a look and laughed.

"What's so funny?"

"Nothing," Aimi said, recovering quickly. "Nothing at all. Want to help me set the table out on the deck?"

"Sure," he said.

Once outside, Aimi set the tray of dishes on the table, then yelped when Jackson grabbed her around the waist. Turning her in his arms, he kissed her, murmuring around her lips.

"Been waiting all day to do this."

Aimi pulled back slightly. "I doubt that, since you've been napping the past two hours and you kissed me just before you went to sleep."

"Then I've been dreaming about doing this."

"Your kisses are pretty dreamy," she said, pulling his head down for more.

"Get a room," Josh said.

"Where'd you come from?" Aimi asked.

"I came through the side gate. Heard our illustrious sheriff was getting his beauty sleep on our couch."

"Ha ha," Jackson said as Dana joined them.

"You're home."

"And glad to be." Echoing Jackson's earlier words, Josh kissed his wife. "Been waiting all day for this." He kissed her again.

"Now who needs to get a room?" Jackson mumbled.

After a dinner alive with conversation, Jackson and Aimi headed back to his house.

"Dinner was fun, wasn't it?" Aimi said.

"It was. Josh and Dana are good people."

"And Dana already looks better than she did yesterday, thank goodness."

Jackson reached for her hand, tucking it into his thigh as he drove. "Do you like boats?"

"Boats?" Aimi couldn't quite wrap her head around the out-of-the-blue question.

"Yeah, you know, those floaty things that go on water?"

"Yes. I like boats, I guess. Why?"

"I signed us up for an ocean charter tomorrow."

"What kind of charter?"

"A fishing boat."

"Oh, I don't know, Jackson. Baiting hooks and gutting fish? I'm not sure that's my thing."

"Well, let's find out. I never really figured you for a girly girl, so I thought it might be fun."

"Thanks," she said dryly. "I don't remember any marina in Willow Bay." She really wasn't thrilled with this idea.

"There isn't one. The charter is out of Westport, about a forty-minute drive from here."

"Couldn't you and Josh go, maybe some other time when we don't have all this stuff hanging over our heads?"

He glanced her way. "Afraid to give it a try?"

"A dare? That's a pretty underhanded maneuver, buddy."

"Did it work?"

"Damn it. Yes. I guess we're giving this a try."

"Good."

Aimi yawned. "I'm sure tired. I don't know why. I slept solid last night, thanks to you." His arms around her had meant the difference between no sleep and the sleep that safety gives you, deep and long.

"That will always be my immense pleasure."

"So what time do we have to leave for the charter?"

Jackson kept his eyes on the road and his hands on the steering wheel. "We, umm, have to be there at 4:30 a.m."

"You've got to be kidding me." Aimi sighed. "You could have told me that before I committed."

"You might not have agreed. I promise you'll enjoy yourself."

"Fine, but I should make you sleep on the couch for omitting that little detail."

"Hey, it's my house."

"Well, it's my couch."

"Okay, okay," he said. "I appreciate that you're willing to give this a try. If this isn't your thing, I will never ask you to do it again."

"I can live with that."

~~~

The next day, Aimi wasn't so sure she *could* live with this. Getting up at 2:30 a.m. had been bad enough, but now she was on a boat so far out she couldn't see land. That was a whole new thing for her, and the waves seemed almost taller than the boat. Up they went, then down, then up again.

"Oh, God," Aimi groaned. She hung her head over the side and heaved up what little was left in her stomach.

Jackson held her hair and patted her back.

When she stood back up, leaning heavily on the railing for balance, she glared at Jackson. "It'll be fun, you said."

"I'm really sorry. I didn't think you would get seasick."

"Yes, and that's why you can't quite wipe that grin off your face, right? Can we go home now?"

The sheepish look on Jackson's face told Aimi she wasn't going to like what he said. "They, umm, don't turn around and head for home until everybody's done catching."

"What? You mean I'm stuck on this boat for hours more?"

"Well, yeah."
~~~

Aimi sank to the deck. "Then you'd better get fishing, buddy, because you've got two limits to catch, and quick."

When they finally got back to land and disembarked, Aimi fell onto a bench, grateful to be done with the rise and fall of Mother Nature's whim. Before long, she was bundled in Jackson's truck with his limit of fish in a cooler in the back.

"Just so you know, I'm not helping you process that when we get home."

"No problem. I've got it."

Aimi barely heard him, surprised she'd referred to his house as home. When had she started thinking of the quaint little craftsman with the modern interior as home? Was it because of the house itself or because of him? Home could very easily become wherever Jackson Smith was. She watched him as he concentrated on the drive, admired his chiseled jaw. His eyes stayed on the road, but the crinkles at their edges made him appear on the brink of a hearty laugh. His hands gripped the steering wheel, not tight but with just the right amount of pressure to maintain control. He had great instincts that way. He seemed to know just how much pressure to apply to any person or situation. And in bed? Oh, God. Those hands were magic, as were his lips.

"Want to stop somewhere for a bite to eat?" he asked quietly.

"Definitely not. I want to go home and crawl into bed."

There was that little quirk of his lip again.

"To sleep, Jackson. To sleep."

His smile was full-on now. "All right. Home to sleep. You got it."

Aimi leaned her head against the window with a grin of her own. Life with Jackson would always be interesting. Her eyes drifted closed.

Pop! Pop!

Aimi came wide awake.

"Duck," Jackson said, pushing her down while swerving back and forth across the road, steering with one hand.

"Were those gunshots?" Aimi said.

"I think… yes. Just stay down. I'll get us home."

~~~

Jackson couldn't believe this was happening again. What was with this guy? Every time the police thought they had a lead, he eluded them. Keeping low, Jackson continued to swerve until they'd gone a couple miles without hearing any more gunshots. He checked the rearview mirror just in time to see a beater truck ram them.

"Oof," Aimi said, still tucked in the footwell.

The hit made Jackson's truck swerve. He turned the wheel into the swerve but didn't quite get them righted before the truck hit them again. This time, they spun in a 360-degree arc. Aimi screamed as Jackson fought the wheel. They came to a stop as the truck raced past them. Jackson barely had time to note the Washington plates before it was gone.

Right now, he was more concerned with his wobbly vehicle. They were precariously positioned near a ravine and every instinct told him not all the wheels were on the ground. Aimi shifted and the truck dipped on her side.

"Freeze. Don't move," he said, his voice urgent.

Thankfully, Aimi froze.

"The truck's off-balance. I think the front passenger tire is hanging over the ravine."

Her eyes widened, but he gave her credit. She didn't move.

"Here's the plan. I'm going to open my door wide. Once it's open, I'm going to take both your hands, then I'll step out, bringing you with me. Got it?"

One curt nod was all the answer he needed.
~~~

Slowly, he opened his door. The truck groaned and pitched a bit, but stabilized. "Okay, ready for this?"

"No, but I have to be," Aimi answered, reaching out both hands to him without hesitation. "I trust you, Jackson."

Her trust touched him. That she followed his directions and had faith in his judgment meant a lot to him. Especially considering she didn't give up control easily. A lump stuck in his throat as emotion welled up. He pushed it down. Now wasn't the time. Keeping eye contact with Aimi, he took her hands and stepped out of the truck. One foot, then, leaning his elbows on the seat, the other foot. Slowly, he pulled Aimi to him, the truck creaking and swaying with the weight change. Finally, when she was lying across the seats, he felt the truck react to the change in weight distribution. He yanked Aimi toward him and out of the truck, and they both fell back onto the asphalt road as his truck listed then rolled into the ravine.

"Shit," Aimi said, clinging to Jackson. "That was close."

"Too close." He couldn't calm his breathing as Aimi's brush with death sank in.

She reached up and turned his face toward her. "You save my life." She kissed him. Once, twice, and finally his world righted itself. "Thank you," she said.

Jackson nodded, the words stuck in his throat. What he felt for this woman went way beyond anything he'd ever felt before. If anything happened to her…

Aimi must have sensed his fear, because she hugged him tightly, burying her head in his chest. "I'm all right. We're all right." Over and over, she repeated the words.

It helped. He sat up, bringing her with him, finally able to draw a deep breath.

"Are you really all right?"

"I think so." She stretched her arms and rotated her shoulders and neck. "I think I'll have a couple bruises and aches, but everything seems to be working all right. You?"

"I'm fine," he said.

She stared at him.

"Okay, not fine. But, like you said, everything's working." Jackson stood and helped Aimi up. Together, they looked over the edge at his truck, smashed against a tree about twenty feet down.

"Damn. I really liked that truck."

"You'll find another. Thank goodness for insurance."

"Oh, man," Jackson said.

"What?"

"We lost the fish. Look. It's spread all over the place."

Aimi chuckled. "No great loss for me. I just want to forget this day ever happened."

They hugged each other, grateful to be alive and together. Jackson pulled his phone out of his pocket and called 9-1-1.

CHAPTER SIXTEEN

"Thanks, Rob," Jackson said.

Aimi waved to him, too tired and sore to talk. She just wanted to lay down, fall asleep, and wake up to a new day. Hopefully having forgotten this one ever happened.

Dana and Josh stood in the doorway of their house, impatiently waiting as Josh and Aimi climbed the steps. They'd decided to stop in because it was on the way and Dana had threatened to haul her pregnant self to Jackson's house if they didn't. She wanted to lay eyes on Aimi to make sure she was okay. Aimi had agreed. She knew she'd feel the same way, and Dana needed her rest.

Dana pulled her into such a tight hug, Aimi grunted in pain.

"Oh," Dana said, lightening up. "I'm so sorry. Are you all right?" Worry shone in her eyes. Her forehead wrinkled with tension and she wouldn't let go of Aimi.

"I'm okay," Aimi said, though the more time passed, the sorer she got. All she wanted was a nice, long soak in a tub, then to crawl into bed.

"Really?" Dana said.

"Really."

"Come in, sit down," Josh said, nudging his wife out of the entryway and gesturing to Jackson to follow.

Aimi sank onto the couch, Dana right beside her. Jackson sat on the arm of the couch on Aimi's other side and she was glad of it. Right now, she didn't want to be anywhere but beside him, the closer the better.

"What happened?" Josh asked.

Aimi leaned into Jackson's thigh. He put his arm around her shoulders as he told the story.

"Do you think Monty shot at you and ran you off the road? Wasn't he driving a silver SUV?"

"Who else could it be?" Aimi said, anger filtering in despite her exhaustion.

Jackson hugged her tighter. "It was a beat-up old truck, but it's hard to believe it could be anyone else."

"This is ridiculous," Dana said, jumping up. "He can't get away with this."

Josh reached for his wife's hand and pulled her onto his lap, placing one hand over her stomach. "Calm down, sweetheart. You're supposed to be taking it easy."

Dana placed her hand over his and stared at Josh for a long moment. Aimi almost looked away from the private communication. Powerful, nonverbal, conversation built out of a strong love. She'd never wanted that before, never really missed it, but now…

She glanced up at Jackson, whose unguarded face evinced such longing that Aimi looked away. Did he want this? With her? The foreign well of emotion that built up in Aimi as she watched Jackson scared her, it was so strong. She loved Jackson. She knew that. The question was, did she love him enough to give over some of the power she'd worked so hard to attain?

This was too much to try to figure out right now. Aimi clutched her head, bringing Jackson's focus back to her. "Headache?"

"A bit," she said. "I think I just need to lie down."

Jackson looked at Josh. "Can you give us a ride home?"

"Sure," he said, helping Dana up, then standing.

Dana hugged Aimi after she stood. "I'm really glad you're not badly hurt, Aims."

"Me, too." Gosh, she loved Dana, the best friend she'd ever had. Aimi hugged her back, tight. "I think we both need to go lay down."

"Which is exactly what you are going to do," Josh said to his wife.

"Yes, Sir!" Dana gave him a mock salute.

Aimi wasn't so sure she could be as nice as Dana about an order like Josh's, even if it did show how much he cared. Once they walked out to the porch, Jackson picked Aimi up. She squirmed in his arms.

"Put me down. I can walk just fine."

"Humor me," he said, his voice low and dusky.

And just like that, she gave in and relaxed. Being carried by Jackson, cared for by him opened the well in her heart that much further. Maybe she could get used to an order or two.

~~~

Jackson lifted a sleeping Aimi carefully from the back seat where he'd held her as Josh drove them home. With a nod of thanks to Josh, he headed to the house, managed to unlock the front door and turn off the alarm, then settled Aimi in bed. As he snugged the cover over her, she sighed, and the sound echoed through him as his heart answered. He'd almost lost her today. God, he couldn't even think the words without quaking in fear. He loved her. There was no denying that now. If anything happened to her, he'd never
~~~

recover. Jackson knelt by the bed and smoothed back Aimi's hair, deciding right then and there that he'd make it his life's work to keep her safe. To make her happy. To show her how much he loved her.

Weary beyond anything he remembered, Jackson went outside and checked the perimeter of his property for signs of tampering. He did the same thing inside the house, then sank down onto the couch, laying his head back and rubbing his face.

How had things become so convoluted? How could one man create so much havoc in their lives? He mentally categorized events. Purse-snatching, property damage to Dana's back door, shots fired at the storage facility, and now more shots followed up by a semi-effective attempt to drive them off the road.

Monty Smoots sure had it out for Aimi. What would make a man go this far? What broke a man this badly? All Aimi's research into the man and her notes on helping Helen Smoots get away from her husband were laid out on the coffee table in front of him. Sitting up, Jackson picked up Aimi's notes and started reading.

Per the designed escape plan, Helen Smoots had left to pick up more beer for her husband, about the only errand he'd allow her to do on her own. She did this even though she could barely walk from the beating he'd given her when he'd run out of beer.

Jackson shook his head but continued reading.

Helen parked their only car in the store parking lot, then got on a city bus to a shelter, where Aimi met her.

In court, Helen Smoots had joined the proceedings virtually, citing fear of retaliation from her husband. Since Aimi had been there in person, she was the only target for Monty's rage. And rage he had, to the point where he'd been thrown in jail overnight to cool down.

After that, Monty had disappeared. No one knew where he'd gone, but the assumption was he'd decided to start a new life somewhere else.

Where has Monty been for the last year? Why did he choose to come after Aimi now? And how does he own such a high-end vehicle? The man hasn't worked in forever, from what I can tell.

Aimi had highlighted these questions and Jackson agreed they needed answering. Where *had* Monty Smoots been? He grabbed a fresh pad and pen, pulled out his phone, and started making calls.

CHAPTER SEVENTEEN

Aimi woke up slowly until she tried to move. Every muscle in her body screamed, popping her eyes open and pulling a groan from her. Right behind the pain came the memories. Fishing. Getting shot at. Almost dying when the truck fell into a ravine.

Being saved by Jackson.

With that last thought, she smiled, then realizing that didn't hurt, the smile widened. Jackson Smith was the real deal. Never one to want to be protected, she could learn to like it from him. The feeling of safety she got when he was around made her go all squishy and soft inside.

She would have loved to lay there thinking about Jackson, but she needed the bathroom, bad. Turning onto her side, not without issue, Aimi pushed up, then had to hold onto the nightstand as a wave of dizziness washed over her. Once that abated, she stood with care, her bladder really leaning on her to get moving. Slowly, one painful step after another, she made it.

Done, she headed downstairs, surprised to see a blanket and pillow folded up on the sofa.

"I didn't want to disturb you," Jackson said, coming in from the kitchen with a steaming cup of coffee in his hand. He set it down and pulled Aimi into his arms, exactly where she wanted to be.

"Good morning, sweetheart," he said, kissing her lustily, but careful not to hurt her.

"Mmmm." Aimi leaned into him. "This is a nice way to wake up."

"Are you very sore?"

"Oh, yes. Definitely sore." She shrugged, but a hit of pain stopped her. "This too shall pass," she said, trying to smile.

"I'll get you some coffee and ibuprofen," he said.

"No, I'll get it. I need to walk around some. It helps."

"Then if you're all right, I'm going to hop in the shower."

"Go. I'll be fine." She pulled him down for one more kiss, then sent him on his way.

After she poured herself a cup of coffee with a dollop of her favorite cream, Aimi grabbed her phone from the island and went out to the couch. Gingerly, she sat down and let out a sigh of relief when her body relaxed into the leather. Maybe she could just lay here and not move for, oh, say, the next week or so?

The shower came on upstairs and a part of Aimi wished she weren't too sore to join him. To distract herself, she looked around. Her papers had been moved, or, more accurately, neatened up. And there were notes scrawled in a man's handwriting. Aimi had never seen Jackson's penmanship before. He definitely wrote like a guy, all strong and in a hurry. She smiled as she looked at it. When her phone rang, she glanced at it before answering, surprised at who was calling.

"Helen?"

"Oh, thank God it's you, Aimi. I've been so worried."

Thinking she'd heard about the accident somehow, Aimi answered. "I'm fine, really. Just a few sore muscles."

"Sore muscles? What happened?"

"Ummm, I thought you knew. Someone tried to run us off the road yesterday."

"Monty?" Her voice, nothing but a whisper, shook in fear.

"Maybe. We don't know yet."

"God, if he finds me… "

"We've managed to hide you for over a year. What makes you think he'll find you now?"

"Someone called."

Aimi straightened, not caring about her aches and pains. Helen was in trouble.

"I didn't know the caller. I'm afraid it was someone Monty pulled into his web." From the way her voice quavered, Helen was near to tears. "I've been packing all morning. I've got to get out of here."

"How could Monty have gotten your phone number?"

"I-I don't know. But somehow, he did."

"Okay, let's look at the facts. Someone called you but it wasn't Monty. What did he want?"

"Information about my life with Monty."

"What kind of information?"

"How long we were married. Did Monty own any property anywhere or have friends who might hide him."

"That doesn't sound like a Monty crony, Helen."

"Who else could it be?" Her voice rose.

Aimi glanced at the notes in front of her. There, repeated from her own notes and scrawled in Jackson's bold writing was the question. *Where has he been?* The shower clicked off upstairs as a distressing idea came to mind.

"Helen, did the man identify himself?"

"Well, yes, but he had to be lying. He said he was some cop from Willow Bay over on the coast. Why would someone all the way over there be calling me and asking questions? It had to be a lie."

"Jackson Smith." Aimi's stomach hit the floor.

"Yes! How did you know that?"

Aimi stared up the ceiling and swore to herself a couple times, then drew a deep breath. "He's legit, Helen. I'm here with him in Willow Bay. He's been protecting me from Monty."

"Oh, my God. Really?"

"Yes. I'm so sorry he scared you." She was going to kill Jackson when she got off the phone. Absolutely bury him. Alive if possible.

"How did he get my number? And if he has it, couldn't Monty get it?"

"I've kept your phone number confidential." Damn. She was going to have to explain more than she wanted to. "Your phone number is in my phone under the first name only. Jackson is very good at figuring things out, and he's gotten pretty protective of me, something we'll be talking about as soon as I get off the phone, I assure you." Aimi glanced at Jackson's notes. "He was trying to solve the same riddle as me. Where has Monty been this past year?"

"D-did he?"

"I don't know, but the questions he asked will help us find him and put him behind bars for a long, long time. Helen, you don't need to move. You're safe. Your contact number is safe. And I'm so, so sorry Jackson scared you like this."

"Oh, gosh, did he ever."

The long breath Aimi heard Helen draw calmed her own nerves as well, though not her anger. "Jackson won't call you again. I swear on my life he won't." *Because I'll be putting the fear of God into him, damn it.* "How about this? I'll call you each day at, say, 4 p.m. and update you on the situation. Sooner, if we catch Monty. Only me. Not Jackson. So if anyone else calls you that's not me, it might well be Monty."

"That would work." Helen let loose with a huffed laugh. "I guess that means I can unpack."

"It sure does."

"I have a good life here, though I'm ready to leave it behind when my friend arrives and we move on together. Still, the thought of leaving now, in a hurry, brought all those old feelings back."

"And once we find Monty, you'll be able to settle permanently wherever you want, Helen."

"Let me know how it goes."

"I will. Take care."

Aimi set her phone down and took a couple deep breaths, trying to calm her elevated heart rate. It didn't help, so with care for her aching muscles, she marched upstairs with as much attitude as she could muster. Jackson had gone too far this time.

~~~

Jackson, still shirtless, reached for his jeans, turning at a noise in the doorway. Aimi stood there, her eyes bright as she stared at him. With a slow smile, Jackson stepped toward her.

"Don't bother," Aimi said, holding up a hand.

The tone of her voice sounded off and a closer look showed the fire of anger in her eyes. Besides, she'd flicked her hair twice already. At him? He yanked his jeans back up and, leaving them undone, went to put his arms around her.

She threw them off and stomped into the room, groaning with every other step.

"What's the matter, Aimi?" he asked.
~~~

"You. You're the matter. How could you call Helen Smoots, Jackson? How could you?"

Confused, Jackson shook his head to clear it, trying to make sense of what Aimi was saying. "Monty's ex-wife?"

"Yes, Monty's ex-wife. You scared the crap out of her."

"How? I identified myself clearly as a sheriff."

"From some Podunk town that should have nothing to do with her case. She thought you were someone Monty told to find out where she was."

Dread filled him. Dread and remorse. He'd scared a woman who'd had more scares in her life than she deserved. "Shit, Aimi. I didn't mean to. I need to call her and apologize."

"You will do nothing of the sort. I've apologized enough for both of us." Aimi marched up to Jackson and poked him in the chest. "The fact that she and I have each other's numbers is a breach of protocol. That you found it, something I'm supposed to guard with my life, makes me seem untrustworthy." She poked him again with each of her next words. "I don't like coming across as untrustworthy. Not. One. Bit."

Not wanting to seem like a wuss, Jackson held his ground, but damn, this woman could put some strength behind that finger of hers. When she turned away, he rubbed the area, sure he'd end up with a bruise. Which was nothing compared to the bruise on his heart. When Jackson wrapped his arms around her. She stiffened.

"I'm sorry, sweetheart. More sorry than I can express. I would never intentionally cause a woman to be afraid. Ever. I'm an ass who didn't think. I needed answers and drove straight ahead with blinders on."

After a long moment, she relaxed back into him. "Yes, you did," she said. Her voice, quieter now, still held a hint of her anger.

"You have every right to be angry, and so does Helen."

"We do, damn it," Aimi said, before letting out a resigned sigh. "How do you manage to do that? To deflate my anger?" She turned and stretched her arms around his neck. "Don't ever do that again, Jackson. We're supposed to be a team, and you can't go using information I gather without at least running it by me."

"Understood. Forgive me?"

He kissed the top of her head, waiting, and grateful beyond belief when she pulled him down for a kiss. "Just don't do it again."

He backed away and crossed his heart.

"You were a boy scout?"

"Made it to eagle."

Aimi rolled her eyes. "God help me. Come on, let's get some breakfast and go over what you put together while I was dead to the world."

Gladly, Jackson thought. Though, watching her ass as she walked out of the room, he wondered if she'd forgiven him enough to do other things in the kitchen first. He hurried after her to find out if make-up sex was really as good as everyone said it was.

CHAPTER EIGHTEEN

Distraction was good, right? Aimi stepped out of the bathroom still vibrating from being sidetracked by Jackson. That man could drive thought straight out of her mind. Even her sore muscles faded beneath his ministrations. When she joined him in the kitchen, he had omelets just about ready to eat. If Aimi had any residual anger, it disappeared as her stomach growled. The man knew how to grovel.

Boy did he. Her body still thrummed with the aftermath of their love-making. Now, as he stood there shirtless and humming some tune Aimi didn't recognize, Aimi contemplated forgoing breakfast altogether.

"Come and eat," Jackson said, his warm smile evidence of his own contentment.

"That looks great," Aimi said, grabbing a chair at the counter. It was kind of nice to have the stove in the island. Jackson was clearly a better cook than her and she liked watching him. The muscles in his arms moved with confidence as he flipped the omelets onto plates.

"Veggie for you," he said, handing her one.

"And ham and cheese for you. Heavy on the ham."

Jackson shrugged. "I need my protein. Especially," he pecked her on the cheek as he sat beside her, "with as much energy as we use up."

"I do love using up energy with you," she said, smiling. "But, maybe we should get back to the problem at hand. Did you find out anything new about the elusive Monty Smoots?"

"Yes, and no," Jackson said around a mouthful of omelet. "I found out why he's been absent this past year, but not where he is at the moment."

"Where's he been?"

"After the divorce and his first attack on you, he spent some time in jail. When he got out, he went on a bender."

"That much, we already knew."

"After that, he spent months searching for Helen. Thank God you hid her well. When he couldn't find her, he went on another bender. Even worse this time. He got drunk, then tried to drive. He ended up putting his car in a ditch, breaking both legs and puncturing a lung. Oh, a concussion, too. He only got out of rehab a few weeks ago."

"I didn't think of hospitals. That's why we couldn't find him."

"Exactly. And he's basically had a lot of time to fuel his hatred. I talked to the social worker on his case while he was in rehab. She wouldn't tell me much because of HIPAA guidelines, but she did mention that the man had quite the temper."

All directed at me. Aimi stared down at her omelet.

"I reached out to someone I know in that area. Police were called to the rehab center on three different occasions because he'd flown into a rage. He discharged himself against medical advice after the last one, which is why he still has a limp."

"I notice you have a bit of a limp, too."

"That noticeable, huh?" Jackson frowned. "I work hard to cover it up."

"And only someone who knows you well would notice it. It's barely there. What happened, anyway?"

"No big story. A football injury. Killed my career."

"Pro?" This was a new factoid about Jackson.

"Barely. First pre-season game and I was out."

"Ouch."

"I don't regret it. I might not be doing what I am today if I hadn't washed out. And I love what I do."

Aimi leaned over and kissed him. "I love what you do, too."

Jackson put an arm across the back of her chair. "If you don't stop looking at me like that, we'll never get anything done."

While Aimi would like nothing better than to spend the day in bed with Jackson, he was right. Catching Monty had to take priority. She sighed.

"All right, then. Back to the subject at hand. So, Monty has a limp." Something bothered her, something she couldn't quite put her finger on. That limp. "Wait a minute. I don't remember the guy who tried to steal my purse having a limp."

Jackson smacked the table, startling Aimi. "That's why he could shoot at us and also be behind to run us off the road. He's got a partner. I should have figured that out long before this."

"Don't be too hard on yourself. Monty seems very good at hiding clues."

"Except now we're looking for two guys who may or may not have been together. Come on." Jackson jumped up, grabbing their plates—with her almost-finished omelet—to put them in the sink.

"Where are we going?"

"We're going to canvas all the hotels and motels in the area."

"We?"

He tucked a strand of hair behind her ear. "Not making that mistake again. We'll do this together, as long as I think it's relatively safe."

Aimi's heart swelled with love for this man. "Thank you," she whispered, hugging him tight.

Two hours later, they pulled into the parking lot of the next hotel on their list.

"This is ridiculous," Aimi said. "This is a tourist town and there are a lot of hotels and motels. It's like trying to find a needle in a haystack."

"Yes, but it's the only haystack we've got. Come on. One more, then we'll head over to Connie's café and I'll buy you lunch."

"Good, since that delicious omelet you made is only a memory and I could really use something to drink."

Jackson grinned his all-out grin and it melted Aimi. She got out of the car and followed him inside the Pacific Lodge.

"Umm, this is pretty upscale. I doubt they'll be here."

"Leave no stone unturned," Jackson quipped as they headed for the front desk.

Five minutes later, they were back in his squad car. Once again, they'd come up empty, so they drove to Connie's retro 50s café and sank into a booth.

"Hi, Jackson," Connie said, handing them menus.

"Hi, Connie. Have you met Aimi Larson?"

"Yep. She ate here when she first got to town."

"I keep coming back for the food and these wonderful, black-and-white checkered floors."

"Did you buy Mike's practice?"

Though her hair was peppered with gray, Connie had very few lines on her face. She managed to stay youthful despite running a café, raising three kids, and having a husband who was out of work more often than not. At least, that's what Dana had told Aimi.

"I did buy Mike's practice," she answered. "He's somewhere sailing the seven seas with his wife by now."

"Good for him." Connie glanced around the restaurant. "Wonder when that time will come for me."

"You're way too young to retire," Jackson said, smiling.

"You sweet-talker, you." Someone nearby waved to Connie. "I'll let you look over the menu. Be back in a minute."

After Connie walked off, there was nothing to stave off their situation. Aimi stared at the menu, not really seeing it. "Why can't we find him?" she asked.

Jackson reached across the table for Aimi's hand. "We will. We've got lots of people keeping an eye out."

"You two ready to order?" Connie asked, rejoining them.

Aimi still hadn't looked at her menu. "Umm, I'll just have a salad, blue cheese on the side, and an iced tea."

With a nod, Connie wrote on her pad. "Lemon?"

"Please."

"Jackson? The usual burger with everything on it and extra fries?"

"That works for me. And coffee."

"Got it."

Connie returned shortly with their drinks. "Why the glum faces, you two?"

"Aimi's being harassed."

That was the understatement of the year. Aimi stirred her ice tea.

"By whom?" Connie asked.

"Some guy is trying to hurt Aimi because he didn't like that she handled his wife's divorce. We just figured out that he's got a partner helping him but we haven't been able to find them."

"One of 'em got a limp?"

Aimi's head whipped up. "Yes."

"The other one swarthy looking?"

"We don't know," Jackson answered. "Have you seen them?"

She nodded. "I think so. They kept watching out the window, weren't happy with the time it took to get their food, and left as soon as they ate. No tip, either. Jerks."

"When?"

"Gosh, just a couple hours ago."

Jackson leaped up and threw some bills on the table. "Cancel that order, Connie. Did you see what they were driving?"

Aimi grabbed her purse and stood up. "And which way they went?"

"Some silver SUV, I think." Connie cocked her head, glancing out the window. "They headed south. I remember because they had a taillight out."

"That's great information," Jackson said, pecking Connie on the cheek.

"That cuts down the places we need to check," Aimi said.

"And if we find their hotel, I'm taking you home and calling for reinforcements."

"One thing at a time," she said, unwilling to go along with that, at least for now.

In moments, they were back in the squad car headed south on the main road. "Let's just drive around for a bit first. See if we can get lucky and spot their car."

An hour later, without a sighting or positive answer at the motels on the south side of Willow Bay, Jackson and Aimi headed back toward the center of town. Aimi stared out the window, unable to fathom how someone could disappear and reappear so often without being seen.

"We'll find him," Jackson said.

"Not soon enough," she mumbled, letting the wasted day get to her.

Jackson pulled over suddenly, causing Aimi to grab the overhead handle and look up. Gladys stood on the side of the road, waving them down.

With a hasty "wait here" in Aimi's direction, Jackson hit the brakes and was out of the car. She rolled down her window.

"I'm glad I found you," Gladys said. "Been looking for a while now."

"What's the matter, Gladys?" Jackson asked. "How can I help?"

"It's how I can help you. I see that attorney is in your car." Gladys waved at Aimi and smiled. "I went by her office and noticed the door was open. Thought she was inside until I glanced in. Place has been redecorated a bit."

Aimi's heart hit her throat. They'd trashed her office? "We need to get over there right away, Jackson."

"Agreed."

"Wait. There's one more thing. I hollered in, and the ruckus I heard made me take a little look around the side. I saw 'em leave. Two guys, both in jeans and flannels, one limping."

Jackson whipped out his phone. "Did the one with the limp look like this?"

While she couldn't see what Gladys was peering at, Aimi assumed it was Monty's picture. "Yeah. Scruffier, though."

"What were they driving?"

"They weren't. They hoofed it, limp and all. Took off toward those old mansions on the north side of town."

Simultaneously, Aimi and Jackson looked in that direction.

"Anything else you can remember, Gladys?" Jackson asked. Aimi knew this was important but she was eager to get searching.

"Nothing I can think of, except there are some nice homes in that area. I'd hate to see these vagrants ransack them."

"I'm on it," Jackson said. "Thank you for the information. You okay? You need a ride anywhere? Money for food?"

Jackson reached for his wallet, but Gladys waved him off. "I'm fine. I don't need anything. This town takes good care of me. Now you go scoot and find those vagrants."

After he shook her hand, Jackson jumped back in the car. Except he didn't take off. He just stared out the front window.

"What are you waiting for? Let's go get them."

"I'm trying to figure out how to say this," he said.

"Because I'm not going to like what you're about to say?"

"Exactly."

"Spit it out, Jackson. We need to get going."

"I need to get going."

I? Oh hell no. "You're not taking those men on alone."

"No, I'm not. But you won't be helping me."

"Over my dead body."

"That's what I intend to prevent." He turned to face her, reaching for her hand. "Aimi, I love you. I don't know when or how, and I wasn't looking for this, but I've fallen. Hard. If I lost you, it would be the end of me."

Her eyes grew wide as she listened to him. Her heart grew too, but she refused to focus on that. "I love you, too, but now's not the time."

"My gut tells me we're closing the net on these guys. I'm taking you to the office. Calling Josh and Paul to come stay with you. And I'm calling backup to help me search for them from here on out."

"I have to be there, Jackson. You can't keep me out of this."

"Why, Aimi? Why do you *have* to be there?"

"I-I don't know. I guess I need to see for myself that Monty won't be after me anymore. I've always been a seeing-is-believing kind of person."

"That's not good enough. I need you safe."

"And I need you safe, too."

"That's why Rob will be with me. He's a good cop, Aimi. Remember, I need to focus on catching Monty and his cohort. If I'm worried about you, that distraction could cost me."

Well, damn. Leave it to Jackson to come up with the one thing that would work.

"Fine," Aimi said. "But I don't like it. Not at all."

"I get that. Thank you. I'm putting the word out, bringing more officers in for this manhunt." Jackson sent three texts, then pulled away, heading to Aimi's office. When they arrived, he went in first and made certain the coast was clear. "It's a mess, Aimi."

"Figured." Still, even with the warning, she almost started crying when she saw how thoroughly the office had been trashed. Papers were everywhere. Rude comments were spray-painted on the walls. Chairs had been ripped and epitaphs had been carved into the wonderful wooden desk Mike had left her.

"Looks like they were inside for a while," she said, hating the wobble in her voice.

"We'll make it good as new once this is over, sweetheart." Jackson put his arms around her. Strong, solid, comforting arms.

She nodded into his chest, telling herself these were just things. No one had been hurt, but still, tears threatened. She willed them away, snuffling and standing back as Rob joined them. Josh and Paul weren't far behind.

"We'll keep her safe," Josh said.

Jackson shook both their hands. "I know you will."

Aimi walked with him to the door. "You keep yourself safe, too, mister."

"I fully intend to." Jackson kissed her. "We're going to get these guys, then you and I are going to have a long conversation about our future. You good with that?"

"I'm very good with that." Aimi hugged him. "Be careful." She included Rob in her glance. "All of you. Monty's got a vicious streak."

As they left, Aimi's heart fluttered against her chest. She put a hand over it, scared to death for Jackson. If anything happened to him…

Josh put an arm around her shoulder and steered her back into the office, closing the door behind him. "How about we clean up some of this mess?"

"I-I wouldn't know where to start." Damn. Wobbly voice was back. "Besides, I can't concentrate while Jackson's out there. I hate not knowing what's going on."

"Good thing I brought my police scanner, then," Josh said. "We can do some cleanup and keep an ear on our guys at the same time."

He set it up. Aimi sank into the chair next to the scanner, listening to the static. "How do we know it's working?"

"It's working," Josh said.

Right then, it squawked. "Dispatch," she heard Jackson's voice. "Run these plates." He read off a number, saying it was a Washington license plate.

Aimi almost hugged the scanner. Meanwhile, Josh and Paul dug out some boxes from the back closet and loaded them up with the loose paperwork that lay on every surface.

"It's going to take you years to sort this all out," Paul said, setting one of the boxes beside Aimi's chair.

"Even worse, most of these files and cases were Mike's." Aimi picked up one sheet, then dug down to look at a few more random pieces. "Thank God."

"What?" Paul and Josh asked at the same time.

"Looks like Mike put a case number on every piece of paper."

"That'll make sorting easier."

After dispatch had identified the license plate as stolen, there'd been no further word on the scanner. Aimi sat bouncing her legs up and down, unable to sit still. Finally, she opened her middle desk drawer and packed the contents into a box. She'd emptied out the last drawer in the damaged desk before the scanner squawked again.

~~~

Jackson and Rob parked behind the stolen vehicle. This shoddy truck parked in an upscale residential neighborhood didn't look right, plus it looked suspiciously like the one that had rammed him and Aimi. They were within a block of Josh and Dana's house. Thank God neither of them was home. Monty and the other guy had to be around here somewhere.

More officers roared in on silent mode and soon they had six men prepared to search. "One house and yard at a time?" Rob whispered.

With a nod and a few jerks of his head, Jackson indicated that the others should go right and he and Rob would go left. They each took a side of the first house and
~~~

met in the backyard, then moved on to the next house, working their way toward Josh and Dana's house. Yard after yard yielded no clues. Until they got to the house next to his friends.

Suddenly, a shot rang out. Jackson froze and zeroed in, listening carefully. The house next to Josh's, the backyard. He signaled to Rob then whipped around the side of the house and through the open gate. Gladys stood at the back gate with what looked like a civil war pistol in her hands.

"That way. They went that way," she hollered, pointing down the alley. "I scared them off."

"Gladys, find cover. This isn't your fight." Jackson whizzed by her and raced down the alley, Rob close on his heels. Ahead, two men were running, one faster than the other.

"Freeze!" Jackson yelled, stopping and sighting his firearm on the one with the limp.

Monty whirled and shot at Jackson and Rob, who both dove for side buildings. His gun still trained in their direction, Monty backed up until he was even with the bushes where his friend had disappeared. Monty fired and the plaster near Jackson's head went flying. He dove for the ground, as did Rob. When they dared a look, Monty was nowhere to be seen. Jackson dusted himself off and signaled to Rob that he'd take point. Carefully, they closed in on the location.

CHAPTER NINETEEN

"Shots fired. Officer down. 611 Vermont Avenue. Ambulance requested."

Shots? Aimi raced out to the reception area where Josh and Paul stood in front of the scanner. She elbowed them out of the way as scanner activity grew.

The words had been so muffled because of the office wall, Aimi didn't know who'd spoken. "Was that Jackson's voice?"

Josh put an arm around her. "No. It was someone else's."

Officer down. Oh, God, did that meant Jackson was the officer down? *Oh, God, oh, God, oh, God.* Aimi turned for the door but Paul blocked her way.

"Let me out. I have to get to Jackson."

"You don't even know where they are," Paul said. "You don't have a car, and you'll only be in the way." Josh took her by both shoulders. "Rob knows we're here. He'll let us know as soon as it's safe. We have to be patient."

"Not my strong suit."

"We'll be right here with you."

Aimi sank onto the chair, trying to sort out all the noise on the scanner and unable to. She sat there, shaking, waiting, unable to breathe. Five minutes passed, then ten, and still no word.

She put her hands together and prayed. She'd finally found love. She couldn't lose it now. *Please.* Jackson was her life. He was larger than life. Willow Bay needed him. She needed him. He just had to be alive. If she lost him, she'd never survive. With clasped hands shaking against her lips, Aimi suffered through more agonizing minutes.

Josh was on his phone but shook his head when Aimi looked up at him. What the hell did that mean? Did he know something and was telling her it was bad or did he not know anything?

The office door opened. Aimi barely heard it, she was so focused on Josh. When his eyebrows rose and he pulled the phone away from his ear, she turned around.

Jackson stood leaning against the open door. Jackson!

"Want to take a ride to the hospital with me?"

His sloppy grin eased the worry out of Aimi and she flew to his side. "Are you all right? I heard the officer down call."

"That was for me," he said, glancing at his leg.

His pant leg had been cut off and his knee was bandaged, though she could see blood seeping through. "What are you doing here? You should be in the hospital."

"Exactly where we're trying to take him, miss," said the paramedic behind Jackson.

"What?" Aimi gawked at her wounded boyfriend. "You came here before going to the hospital?"

He cupped her cheek. "I knew you'd worry."

"Oh, my God. I love you so much for that, but are you insane?" She looked at the paramedic. "Do you have an ambulance to take him in?"

The paramedic nodded at the same time Jackson said "I don't need an ambulance. Aimi can drive me."

"The hell I will," Aimi said. "Come on." She circled a finger in the air and pointed, ordering him without words back out the door. It surprised her that he cooperated.

Josh, grinning, handed her purse and phone to her. "Take care of our guy."

"I intend to." Aimi climbed in the back of the ambulance with Jackson. When the paramedic looked like he would say something to her, she gave him her best courtroom stare. He climbed in behind her.

"No lights and siren," Jackson said. "Got it?"

The paramedic smiled. "Got it. Now lay down, sheriff," the paramedic said. "I need to get an IV started and get your vitals."

"This is embarrassing. I am not lying down."

Aimi turned her stare on Jackson. For a long moment, they locked gazes. With a resigned shake of his head, he lay down.

"That's what I get for stopping."

"Yes, it is. You are going to follow doctor's orders."

"He's not a doctor."

"You know what I damn well mean." Aimi crouched down beside him and reached for his hand. "I was so afraid, Jackson. If I lost you…"

Jackson pulled their entwined hands to his lips and kissed her knuckles. "You couldn't lose me. You're stuck with me. For life. And it's over. You're safe."

Aimi's heart filled with joy over his words, but she filed them away for another day's discussion. "You got shot, Jackson."

"It's just a flesh wound."

"Not with all that blood, it isn't."

Jackson sighed and relaxed back onto the stretcher, throwing his free arm over his forehead. "And in my bad knee, too." He grimaced.

"I know. But it could be so much worse."

Finally starting to let go of her fear, Aimi sank to the floor of the ambulance while the paramedic went to work. She refused to let go of Jackson's hand, though. When the paramedic asked her to, she pulled out the stare again. He moved to the other side to start the IV.

"Smart choice," Jackson said.

"That glare of hers is wicked."

"Don't I know it?"

"And don't you forget it," she said with no steam behind her words. Everything she'd wanted in life, that she'd never known she wanted, had almost gone down in a flame of gunfire.

"I was so scared," she mumbled.

"I'm still here, sweetheart. You can't get rid of me that easily."

"I don't want to get rid of you. Ever." There it was again, that forever talk, and this time, she said it. They really needed to have a long discussion. Forever was something she'd never considered before. Did forever work? She'd been working divorces for so long, she'd become jaded about marriage. And look at people like Helen, stuck in a marriage that almost killed her because of a piece of paper.

"I'm going to give you something for the pain, sheriff."

Jackson nodded, which told Aimi more than anything that he was hurting.

"Might make you a little drowsy." The paramedic fed pain meds through the IV.

"Jackson?"

"Hmmm?"

Apparently, the pain meds were already working.

"What happened to Smoots and the guy helping him?" Aimi asked. She'd completely forgotten about him in all the brouhaha.

"We apprehended his accomplice. Some vagrant he'd hired. As for Monty, he won't bother anyone ever again."

"Jail?"

"Grave."

"Good." It should bother Aimi that she was glad Monty was dead, but it didn't. He never would have stopped. "I'll have to let Helen know."

"Yep. She's free. We all are, thank goodness." His last words were slurred as the meds took full effect.

Aimi stayed on the floor, rocking and rolling at the vehicle's whim as she held tight to Jackson's hand, all the way to the hospital in Aberdeen.

~~~

"It's a through and through," Dr. Stone said after looking at the X-rays. "Not much to do here but wrap you up and send you home."

"Good," Jackson said, about done with being poked and prodded. He'd barely woken up when they got to the hospital due to the meds, so had refused more. He wanted his wits about him. "Does that mean I can go home now?"

"Yes, but you'll need to get a CT and follow up with your orthopedic doctor. And I want you non-weight bearing until you get clearance from him. We'll get you some crutches. Things look a little dicey around those ligaments. It's hard to tell what going on because of your prior injury and surgeries."

"Crutches? I can't do my job if I can't walk on the leg," Jackson said.

"If you don't take the time now to deal with this injury the right way, you might lose the ability to do your job permanently."
~~~

"Oh, he'll do what he's supposed to do, doctor. I'll see to that," Aimi said.

"The entire town will see to that," Josh added.

"What is this? A party?" Jackson growled.

Josh shrugged. "If you want. Right now, it's just me. I figured you'd need a ride home, so after Paul and I figured a way to lock the office up, I came here."

"Thank you," Aimi said. She hugged him.

Jackson grunted, surlier than he knew he should be. Willow Bay only had one resident sheriff. If he had to take days or weeks off, it would make life a lot harder for Rob and the others in the area.

"And don't worry about your job, Jackson," Josh continued. "Rob said to tell you they've already got your shifts covered while you're recuperating."

"See? It's all turning out fine." Aimi's smile lit up the room and almost lifted Jackson's foul mood, but he didn't like being helpless or even down for the count. He was the strong one.

Aimi smoothed his forehead with her hand. "Don't worry," she said for his ears only. "I'll take good care of you."

Getting lost in her eyes, Jackson's mood faded. Almost. Maybe being taken care of wouldn't be so bad, for a little while.

"All right, Doc. I'll follow orders."

Another long, impatience-inducing hour passed, and he endured a very painful transfer to Josh's SUV before they were headed home. Jackson regretted refusing the pain meds now. The knee hurt like a son of a bitch.

"Here," Aimi said, turning around from the front seat. She put a pill in his hand and handed him a water bottle. "Pain med."

"No. The last one knocked me out. You'd have to carry me inside the house."

"You are a lightweight when it comes to pain meds. But this isn't as strong as what the paramedic gave you." She held out her hand again. "Take it. You're in pain. We'll make sure you get into the house and settled. This will help you."

Not sure she was right, but wincing as they went over a bump in the road, Jackson dutifully took the pill and closed his eyes.

"Jackson," Aimi said quietly. "Time to wake up."

He must have nodded off. Jackson opened his eyes and looked around. He was still stretched out in the back of Josh's SUV.

"We're home," Aimi said.

Home. That sure had a nice ring to it.

"Think you can walk inside?"

Well, he damn sure wasn't going to be carried in. He nodded, slowly scooting toward the door. Aimi held his leg until he'd perched on the edge of his seat. Josh handed him the cursed crutches.

"Slow and easy getting up. You haven't been on crutches for years, right? And you're still foggy from the meds."

Holding onto the door, Jackson stood. And swayed. Everything looked a bit blurry.

"Whoa there, my friend," Rob said from beside him.

Dana waited up on the porch. Was the whole town here to witness his weakened condition? Jackson stewed, but took the crutches. Then, with Josh on one side, Rob on the other, and Aimi following closely behind, he wobbled his way up the steps and into the house. He headed for the couch.

"Uh uh," Aimi said. "Straight up to bed for you."

"I'm not an invalid. You're having a fucking party at my expense and I'm damn well going to visit for a while."

"That's our cue," Josh said, reaching for his wife's hand. "We're outta here."

"Me, too," Rob said following them out the door. He paused and turned to Aimi. "Need any help getting this lug up the stairs?"

Jackson scowled, but Aimi only laughed. "I think we can manage."

With a wave, Rob was off to his car.

"See, no more party. Now off to bed with you, mister."

"Hmmm." Jackson didn't argue. He was more tired than he'd been in a long time.

Once settled, with his leg up on pillows, he recognized Aimi's wisdom. "This does feel better."

"Told you so."

"Want to join me?" He toyed with one of the buttons on her blouse as she leaned over him fussing.

"Definitely, but not for that reason. I've got a few things to do, then I'll come cuddle."

A bit miffed, Jackson forgot all about it when she kissed him. Her kisses did that to him. Soft and comforting, she reminded him with her lips to relax, to be at ease. He would be okay.

He closed his eyes and drifted off.

CHAPTER TWENTY

Jackson woke to Aimi's soft body snuggled tight against him, his arm holding her close. It was the best feeling in the world, waking up next to her. He loved her more than life itself and prayed he could start every day for the rest of his life like this.

When he shifted, pain shot from his knee straight to his head and yesterday's events filtered back into his brain.

Aimi sat up, wiping sleep from her eyes. "I'll get you a pain pill."

"No." He pulled her back down to him. "It's easing already and I just want to enjoy laying here. With you."

"Gladly," she said, snuggling back into him.

They lay that way, not talking, just enjoying each other. He dozed off again. When he next became aware, she wasn't in bed.

"Hey, sleepyhead," Aimi said, walking into the room.

He must have really been out of it because her hair was wet from a shower and she was dressed.

"Are you awake enough for company?"

"Definitely," he said, pulling the covers aside for her.

Aimi laughed. "Not me, silly. Paul and Bernie are here to see you. He barely kept her at home last night. She wanted to tear over here and make sure you were all right with her own eyes."

"Oh." He tried to hide his disappointment, but apparently didn't do a very good job because she laughed again.

"You must be feeling better if that's all you can think about."

"That's what you do to me," he said with a chuckle. "I tell you what. Ask them to make themselves comfortable, then come help me put some clothes on. I need to get out of this bed and feel a little more human."

"You've got it." Aimi disappeared but quickly returned, digging in his drawers until she found basketball shorts and a t-shirt.

It took some work, but they managed to get him presentable. He crutched his way down to the living room, surprised that the party of two had turned into a real party. Another one. Josh and Dana were there, as well as Rob. They'd pulled the kitchen stools into the living room to augment the couch.

"You told us to make ourselves at home," Bernie said. "So we answered the door." She hugged Jackson carefully, then backed off until he managed to settle on the sofa.

"Good to see you up without your face scrunched up in pain."

"Sheer will," Jackson said. "I think it hurts worse, if that's possible."

"I bet."

"I haven't had a chance to tell you this yet, but you have a CT on Monday in Aberdeen and we'll drive up to Seattle Tuesday to see your ortho doc." Aimi fluffed the pillow behind him.

"Efficient, aren't you?" Jackson said, pulling her down to sit beside him.

"Yes, I am."

He kissed her, wishing no one else was here so he could do more. To distract himself, he turned to Rob. "My shifts are covered?"

"Totally," Rob said. "We've got a loaner from Benton County checking out life on the coast. Might transfer out here, so he's working with Steve and I'm covering Willow Bay for now."

"Steve and Rob cover the Aberdeen area," Jackson told Aimi, who nodded.

"Hungry?" she asked.

"Actually, I am." Jackson rubbed his stomach.

"Good, because we have a lot of food."

"How?"

"People have been dropping things off all morning. They must think I can't cook," Aimi said.

Bernie laughed and got up. "I'll help you, and it's not that they think you can't cook. They're just showing their love for our sheriff."

Dana joined them. They all headed into the kitchen to put together plates of food.

"How are we standing legally?" Jackson asked.

"You're officially on a medical leave of absence," Josh said.

"I'm not talking about that. What about the Monty thing?"

"Well," Rob said, "there are still a few t's to cross and i's to dot. The oversight board wants to interview Aimi, but I got them to hold off until tomorrow." He shrugged. "It's pretty cut and dried, but there will be the usual inquiry."

Jackson nodded. Standard procedure. "Why do they need to talk to Aimi?" He didn't like that she'd have to relive the whole thing. He'd explained everything that happened, leaving out the gory details. Of course, she'd pulled each and every one of them out of him anyway, but still, rehashing it couldn't be good.

"Filling in backstory. They may want to talk to the ex-wife, too."

"Only with Aimi's permission." Jackson had been on the receiving end of that situation. Never again.

The women joined them, handing out plates of food to everyone.

"This is a lot of food."

"And not half of what we've got in the fridge. It's crazy how much food has been delivered." Aimi held out a hand to Jackson. "Pain pill."

He shook his head. "I don't want to sleep the day away."

"Good thing this is just ibuprofen then."

She knew him well, he thought as he swallowed the pill. "What I'd really like is a cup of coffee."

"Gotcha covered right here," Dana said, handing him a full mug.

"Bless you," Jackson said, sniffing the strong aroma. Perfect.

As the day passed toward evening, so many folks stopped by to see for themselves that Jackson was all right that they'd opted to leave the door open and let people walk in without knocking. By late afternoon, Jackson had about had it with visitors.

"You should go lay down and get that knee up," Aimi said, taking the ice pack off.

"I've got it up."

"Sitting on the couch with your knee on a pillow doesn't qualify. You need to get it above your heart to keep the swelling down. And you have to still be tired from everything."

"I am. Maybe you're right."

"Yoohoo!" came from the front porch.

Jackson and Aimi eyed each other. "Gladys?" Aimi asked.

She peeked her head inside. "Oh, good, you're decent." She walked in and plunked down in the chair next to Jackson. Putting a hand on his shoulder, she looked him over. "I just had to come see with my own eyes that you're all right, young man."

"I am. Not perfect, but healing. Please tell me you didn't walk all the way over here with the dark coming on just to find that out."

"Heavens no. That nice young sheriff brought me."

Rob joined them. "Been waiting on the porch. Figured you were tired of seeing my mug, but I couldn't resist when I ran into Gladys and she bemoaned the fact that she couldn't see you in person."

"You sure my cart is okay, young man?" she asked Rob. "Mabel's my life, you know."

"Dana's got it in her back room at the shop. You know she'll guard it with her life."

"That she will. She's good people. As are you, Aimi Larson. Looks like you're taking good care of our boy here." Gladys stood.

"Are you leaving?" Jackson asked.

"Yep. Now that I've checked on you, I don't want to overstay my welcome. You're looking a bit fatigued, sheriff."

He was, not that he would admit it.

'We've got a lot of food here, Gladys. Can you stay long enough to have a plate?"

"Oh, no, dearie. But I'd surely take one to go."

"Me, too," Rob said.

"You have been in and out all day, man, and munching each time you stop by," Jackson said.

"Yeah, and I'm hungry again. I used up a lot of calories wrestling that cart inside, Rob said, as he walked with Aimi and Gladys to the kitchen, "I don't know how you manage to push it around. That thing is heavy!"

Gladys held up an arm like a bodybuilder. "Muscles, young man. Seems like you could use a few more of them."

Jackson's hearty laugh felt good. They'd been under such a shadow lately, it had been a while since he'd laughed like that.

To-go boxes in hand, Gladys and Rob said goodbye. For the first time in hours, Jackson and Aimi were alone in the house. Aimi put the food away while Jackson enjoyed the simple pleasure of domestic activity. It felt good with Aimi here. He hoped, when the time was right and he asked her to stay, she'd say yes.

"Come on," Aimi said, locking the front door. "Let's go take a nap."

"Yes!" Jackson pumped air.

"To rest and sleep."

"Damn." His brain knew she was right. He was exhausted. But other parts of him…

"Here's a pain pill," she said once they'd made it up the stairs.

"I don't want to be foggy."

"And I don't want you to be foggy, but you need sleep. I'll be right here. Take the pill."

He did. As she joined him, he thought about how well they fit together. They drifted off to sleep, the most natural thing in the world for him. For them.

Some time later in the darkness, he woke to a noise. Whimpering. "Aimi?"

She lay on the other side of the bed. He could tell she was crying.

"Aimi, come on," Jackson said. He tried to turn to her but was stopped by a stab of pain.

"Stop moving," she said quietly. "You'll only hurt yourself."

"Then don't make me come to you."

He waited a few moments and finally, she turned to him, sniffling.

"What's the matter?"

"I-I don't know. I'm usually such a strong person, but I just can't stop c-crying. Or shaking."

Jackson pulled her in tight to his side. "Considering what you've been through, I'm surprised this hasn't happened more."

"I woke up scared to death for no reason and now I can't calm down. I'm better than this. And I need to be strong for you. You're the one who got hurt."

He ran his hand along her back as far as he could. "Sweetheart, you are just about the strongest person I know. You should have broken down numerous times over the last few days and you held it together."

"Not by much."

"But you did it. This kind of reaction is normal after what we've been through."

She sniffed again. "Haven't seen you blubbering like an idiot."

"I'm a little more used to it than you are." He kissed the top of her head.

For the rest of the night, he held her. Eventually, she stopped shaking, then crying, and calmed down. When her breathing had evened out, Jackson finally closed his eyes and drifted back to sleep himself, assured that all was right in his world.

CHAPTER TWENTY-ONE

Aimi woke to sunshine streaming in the window. Jackson had large windows in his bedroom and she loved waking up to the brightness of a sunny day, especially next to him. They'd managed to sleep through the night.

No, wait. They hadn't. She'd woken up, totally freaked out, and had tried to move away from Jackson so he could sleep, but the man heard everything.

Having done some volunteer work at women's shelters, Aimi knew about PTSD. Logic dictated that she would feel the effects for a while. The only way past it was through it. Not necessarily reliving it, but putting it in the right context. And Jackson had helped her do just that last night. Aimi smiled. He'd held her with such tender care. She'd fallen asleep with him whispering in her ear. She had no idea what he'd said, only that his voice made her feel safe.

Carefully, trying to let him sleep, she slipped out of bed. Downstairs in the kitchen, she brewed coffee and leaned against the counter, letting the strong smell wake her up.

Her phone jingled. Dana.

"Hi," she said.

"Hey. Not too early to call, is it? I was hoping you both would get some sleep."

"We did." Thanks to Jackson's calming presence.

"How are you doing?"

Dana was the one person Aimi could be honest with. So she was. "I woke up happy, which is more than I can say for the middle of the night. It all hit me, Dana. I freaked out. Jackson held me until I calmed down."

"That man loves you."

"I think so. I know I love him. I wasn't looking for it, but he barged right into my heart and shredded all my concerns and doubts."

"I'm happy for you, Aims. You deserve a man as good as Jackson."

Maybe she did, maybe she didn't. Aimi knew she'd spend the rest of her life trying to live up to the larger-than-life person he was.

"What's on your agenda today?" Dana asked.

"I have to meet a couple officers at the station for questioning. With Jackson's truck totaled and my car still at the office, I'm not sure how I'll get there."

"Why don't I take you to get your car. I can drop Josh off and he can hang with Jackson while you're gone."

Aimi chewed her lip. "That would work, but Jackson won't like being babysat."

"Let Josh deal with that. What works for you, timewise?"

"Ummm, a couple hours? I have to meet them at noon."

"Okay. Eleven it is."

A groan emanated from upstairs.

"Oops, I think Jackson's awake. I bet he's trying to get up by himself. Gotta go."

"All right. I'll see you at eleven."

Sure enough, when she got to the bedroom, Jackson was sitting on the side of his bed, one hand on his knee, the other keeping him from falling off.

"Dizzy?"

"Yes," he growled.

"In pain?"

"Again, yes." His lips were thin lines.

Aimi brought him his crutches and he hobbled into the bathroom.

"Need help?"

"No, damn it. I can do this much by myself."

Yikes. Someone woke up on the wrong side of the bed. Aimi took the opportunity to change the sheets and open the blinds and windows to freshen up the room. When Jackson hobbled back out, he looked white as a sheet. Aimi helped him into the wing-back chair near the window, then went and got him two ibuprofen, which he swallowed without complaint.

"This hurts more than when I blew out my knee."

"Well, a metal projectile tore through everything. Of course, it hurts more."

He leaned his head back and stared out the window. "I'm anxious to hear what the ortho has to say."

"Me too. Umm, in the meantime, I need to leave for a while."

That brought him around to look at her. "The police interview?"

She nodded, and Jackson started to get up.

"What are you doing?"

"I'm going with you."

"No, you're not." She nudged his shoulder until he sank back into the chair. "You were white as a sheet just going to the bathroom. You'll never make it to the station."

"I will. I have to."

Aimi squatted down beside the chair and put her hands on his arm. "Josh, this is in my wheelhouse. I can handle this."

"You broke down last night. I don't want you to have to go through that again."

"I'm so grateful you were there to help me through that. I feel better this morning, stronger. Because of you."

"Exactly why I need to be with you."

"Knowing you'll be here to come home to, will help." She reached up to brush the creases from his forehead.

"I'm supposed to be the strong one," Jackson said.

"You are, and you'll be back to that eventually. Once your knee heals. Though, I daresay, we have some tussles ahead of us over who gets to do what."

He smiled, relaxing, bringing his arm around her and pulling her in for a kiss. "I look forward to it, Aimi Larson."

"As do I. Now, I need to get ready. Are you all right here?"

"I'll sit here until the meds take effect. I could use a cup of coffee."

"Coming right up."

After delivering the coffee, Aimi went into the bathroom to dress for her interview. There was no way Jackson carried any fault in Monty's death. He'd outlined it all for her. But just in case, she texted Dana to come a few minutes early. She wanted to go to the shop and change into her legal attire. Aimi planned to meet them on even footing, no matter how much power they thought they had.

When Josh walked through the door at the appointed time, Jackson had managed the stairs. "What the hell are you doing here?"

"It's good to see you, too, buddy."

Aimi picked up her purse. "Josh is going to hang here while Dana takes me to get my car and go to the station."

"I don't need a babysitter."

She looked him square in the eye. "Says the man who almost fell out of bed this morning."

"Almost," he answered, giving as good a stare as he got.

"Humor me," Aimi said, then, not waiting for an answer, scooted out the door.

"I don't envy Josh," she said as she got in Dana's car and gave her a hug.

Dana chuckled. "He can handle Jackson."

"I suppose he can. So, how are you feeling?"

"So much better. The meds they put me on really helped. And I'm eating more, which makes my doctor happy. And Josh." Dana pulled out into the street and headed for Aimi's office.

"He's been pretty worried."

"I know, but maybe now we can actually enjoy this pregnancy."

"I hope so."

"Are you ready for the inquisition?"

"I will be. I almost hope they try to press me. I can give as good as I get in court, so I'm looking forward to the fun."

"Good." Dana pulled up behind Aimi's car. "Let me know how it goes, okay?"

"Will do." Aimi got out and dug up her car keys. Glancing at the office, she saw that Paul and Josh had apparently put a new lock on the door. She'd have to get the keys from them so she could get back to work.

On her own for the first time in a while, Aimi couldn't decide if she liked it or not. Having been on her own since she'd gone off to college, it now felt strange to be alone. Willow Bay had done that to her, made her crave family. Jackson had done that.

Smiling, she got in the car and headed for her back room at Tangerine Treasures. Half an hour later, she was ready.

She twirled back and forth in her court suit, a fitted skirt that was lower than femme fatale but higher than pompous, in a gorgeous shade of deep blue. Matching suit jacket, and a crisp white blouse to set it all off. Black heels that met the same standard as her suit. It had been a few weeks since she'd worn heels, so she hoped she could pull this off.

She'd put her hair up in a neat bun and applied makeup. Everything about her said, "Yes, I'm a woman who means business."

Ready, she locked up and drove the few blocks to the sheriff's office, exactly five minutes late.

"You're late," a suited man said as she walked into the station. Aimi waved to Rob and he smiled and waved back.

"Aimi Larson, meet Detective Jordan. Detective Grassi is in the interview room already. They're heading up the investigation into the shooting of Monty Smoots."

"It's nice to meet you, detective." She shook his hand. "Shall we get the ball rolling?"

Two hours later, Aimi stood at the front counter and watched the detectives get into their car and drive off. Rob brought her a bottle of water and leaned against the counter next to her.

"How'd it go?"

"Oh, the usual." She frowned. "I understand the need for these investigations, but I don't get why they have to feel so confrontational. Well, I do, actually. With everything that's going on in the world, they need to clearly understand each situation."

Rob nodded. "Doesn't make it much fun."

"No, but it's done and they'll clear Jackson of any wrongdoing. He acted in self-defense."

"Exactly what I told them."

Aimi glanced at her watch. "Oh, I'd better get back. Jackson is probably chomping at the bit to know how it went and he's probably about to hog-tie Josh to the table and come looking for me. Two hours to ask a few questions. Crazy."

"Tell him everything's under control and to take his time healing."

"I will. Getting him to do exactly that will be the hard part."

"Let me know how it goes at the doc's, okay?"

"I'll have Jackson call you afterward. Otherwise, I'm giving out privileged information."

Rob laughed as he opened the station door for her. "Once a lawyer, always a lawyer."

"Most assuredly." Aimi was still chuckling when she got in the car.

Driving back to Jackson's house, Aimi wondered again at all the changes in her life since she'd come to Willow Bay. Most of all, with Jackson. She'd gone from being controlled most of her growing-up years to the freedom of college life to a stuffy, testosterone-infused, all-male law firm where they'd tried to dominate her. After that attorney had attacked her, she'd sworn to never again give control to someone.

Then she met Jackson, whose life was all about control. She'd fought her attraction to him for just that reason, and now, it just didn't seem as important as it used to. Jackson, one of the strongest men she knew, considered her opinion. Well, mostly. And maybe not at all right now, but that's because he was out of his element with the injury. He listened to her, and sometimes they did things her way, sometimes his.

Wasn't that what a relationship was supposed to be like? Aimi smiled, knowing she wanted more than anything to take the time to find out. She sped up, wanting to get home to Jackson as soon as possible.

Jackson Smith was the best man in the world. From the moment she'd laid eyes on him at Dana and Josh's wedding, she'd been attracted to him. As she got to know him, she'd slowly peeled back the armor to see a true knight, ready to stand beside her, accepting—though not easily—her right to make her own choices.

Her phone rang and, since she didn't have a hands-free setup, she let it go to voicemail. She'd be home in ten minutes anyhow. Exactly where she wanted to be.

~~~

Jackson punched the red button on his phone and threw it across the sofa. "They can't still be questioning her. Where is she?" He should have gone with her. Hating that he'd lost all control of the situation, he punched the back of the sofa.

"Calm down there, Bucco," Josh said. "Aimi has proven over and over again that she can take care of herself."

"She shouldn't have to. I should be there with her."

"And do what? Sit in the outer office waiting? They wouldn't let you inside the interview room. You're the one whose reputation is on the line."

Damn it all. There were times when Jackson hated logic and this was one of them. "Doesn't make me feel any better." He huffed out a couple breaths. "I need some activity."

"Uh, what kind," Josh said with wary eyes.

"Nothing your wife's best friend won't approve of. I just need to walk around a bit. Focus on something else for a moment, or try to."

"That, I can get behind." Josh held the crutches while Jackson stood and got his bearings. But when he tried to follow him, he got a hand to the chest.

"I can walk around just fine. I'm not on the woozy meds except at night. And you can freaking see me from anywhere. It's one big room."
~~~

Josh laughed and plopped back into the chair. "Okay, Bucco, you're on your own."

Jackson made it around the kitchen island twice, then got a glass of water and stood at the sink looking out the window. He really should be working on the yard with all the nice weather. Except that wouldn't happen now that he was gimped up. Next year would have to be soon enough. Maybe he and Aimi could plan a yard remodel together. The idea made him smile. He could see them living here, designing things in a way both of them loved, bringing a family into the house and making it a home.

For all that to happen, she first needed to be done with this interview and back home. He glanced at his watch. Two and a half hours. Wow. This was a cut-and-dried situation. What could possibly take this long?

Intent on not bungling with the crutches, Jackson headed around the island and back into the living room. When he looked up, there she was, leaning against the doorway. With the sun behind her, she looked like an angel. His angel. In a gorgeous lawyer suit that set his fantasies to going wild.

"You're home."

"I'm home," Aimi said, walking straight to him for a hug. Jackson let the crutches fall and hugged her right back.

"Well, now that you're here, I'll just slip on out," Josh said from behind them.

Jackson barely heard the door shut. He tipped Aimi's head up and leaned down to kiss her, letting his heart pour into the kiss, showing her how much he loved her, cherished her. Her arms tightened around him, her lips moving in concert, opening, letting him in, giving herself over to him.

He loved her so much it hurt. "Ouch." He broke the kiss.

"What?" Aimi said, her eyes still clouded with desire.

"I think I forgot myself and put weight on my leg."

Aimi, full of concern, handed him his crutches and mother-henned him until he was back on the couch with his leg up.

"I'm fine, Aimi."

She sat on the edge at his hip. "I need you to be better than fine."

"I will be."

"I'll be anxious until after we see the doctor on Tuesday."

"Right now, I'm trusting what the ER doc said. The rest, we'll figure out when we have to. How was the interview?"

Aimi waved off-handedly. "The usual grilling."

"Ah, damn. I'm sorry you had to go through that. I should have been with you."

"Thinking of you sitting in the lobby in pain would not have helped me." Aimi lay over his chest and snuck her hand under his shirt, running her fingers through his chest hair. Which felt sensual and sexy and made things come alive that probably shouldn't right now.

Jackson placed a hand over hers with the t-shirt between them. "You're making me think of things we could be doing, especially in that sexy suit you've got on."

"Oh, you think you might not be able to perform with a gimp leg?"

"Something like that."

"We can be uber-careful, you know." Aimi stood, pulled the pins out of her hair so it fell free, and took off her jacket. She unbuttoned her blouse, slipping it off and leaving only a sheer white lace to cover her dusky, hardened nipples.

"Come here," he said, his voice husky with desire.

First, Aimi yanked his sweats down, then she hiked her skirt up and straddled him.

"Oh, my God, you don't have panties on."

Aimi smiled, a slow, come-hither smile. "I may have taken them off in the car before I came inside."

"You are the woman of my dreams," Jackson said, cupping her breasts. He ran his thumbs over the nipples and his cock jerked when she groaned with pleasure.

"Bra. Off," he growled.

"Your wish is my command." The bra quickly joined her other clothes on the floor.

"Is the front door locked?"

"I don't think so. Josh went through the door last."

"We'll just have to pray no one barges in then." Without further ado, Jackson took a breast in his mouth, kneading the other one with his hand. Her perfect, perky breasts. He could spend forever showing them attention and never grow tired. He kissed around and under, then pulled the nipple into his mouth. Aimi gasped, and he jerked again.

"Woman, I love your sounds."

She raked his hair with her hands. "Is that all you love?"

"Absolutely not," he said. "I love everything about you from that silky hair down to those painted toenails. And everything in between."

"Some of that in-between stuff wants more attention," she said, her breath quickening.

Jackson kissed her, moving his lips over hers with tender care, though she quickly decided she wanted none of that and deepened the kiss. He let her. He followed her into a world all theirs. The feel of her lips moving across his jaw, down his throat, was heady and filled him with need.

When her lips descended to his nipples, it was Jackson's turn to gasp.

"Do you think," Aimi said, raising her head, "you can keep your leg still and give over control to me?"

"Sweetheart, I think we're way beyond the questioning stage." Using his good leg, he arched toward her core.

"You relax, buster, or this isn't going to happen."

"Yes, ma'am," he said with a grin, tweaking her nipples and enjoying the dark desire in her eyes.

Aimi rose up, then slid over his tip, freezing there, causing Jackson to groan. He reached for her waist, but she grabbed his hands and placed them on her breasts. "That's as far as these hands go, mister. I've got this."

"You've got me. Heart and soul."

"Ditto, my love." She settled down onto him until he was fully sheathed.

"God, you feel so good," she said, gasping. "I love you so much." She rose, then slid back down. Back and forth, slow and measured, driving Jackson nuts. He fingered her nipples, pulling her forward so he could cover them with his mouth. She was his everything.

Again, she held herself with just his tip embedded.

"Aimi!" he growled.

She sank down, quickly this time, increasing the tempo. Jackson reached for her waist.

"Uh uh. You lay perfectly still."

"Ah, damn, woman. You're killing me."

"But what a way to go."

The rate of her breathing increased with his, the time for talking done. She sat up straight and quickened her pace. Jackson reached down between them. When he flicked his finger against her, Aimi screamed her release, her entire body shaking with the love they shared. Jackson followed right behind, unable to stop himself from arching into her as he filled her.

For several long, gasping moments they lay there, suspended in the afterglow of the most amazing release Jackson had ever felt. When Aimi collapsed on top of him, he held her tight to his chest and ran his hand through her hair. "I love you, Aimi Larson." He tipped her head up so she could see his eyes, see the truth there. "Marry me."

Aimi's eyes widened. Would she turn him down? Was it too soon? Jackson chafed as she made him wait. Then, slowly, a smile spread across her face. "Yes. We barely know each other, but yes. I want to marry you more than anything I've ever wanted."

"You've just made me the happiest man in the world, sweetheart." And he kissed her, proving his words with every caress of his lips.

CHAPTER TWENTY-TWO

One month later.

"He put our son in jail," the mother said. "No eight-year-old should see the inside of a jail. Irreparable harm has been done and we believe compensation is due."

"Unless they commit a crime," Jackson mumbled under his breath, which earned him a thigh pinch under the table from his illustrious attorney. He had to pull back the grin itching for release. Nothing could make Jackson feel bad today. He was off the crutches and well on his way to healed. Aimi wore a diamond they'd picked out together while in Seattle for a doctor's appointment. And their house had become a home, with her furniture and a few extra things they'd picked out together. He'd turned domestic and didn't mind one bit. Hell, he even liked shopping with her.

This lawsuit was the last thing keeping him from being completely happy. He just wanted it over with, but even with this hanging over his head, he just couldn't stop smiling.

It didn't help that the mediator, James Claffin, whom Jackson knew from various arrests and testimonies, was trying to keep his own smile under wraps. As was Josh, there to represent Willow Bay.

Aimi responded. "My client was with your son at all times. He never left him alone. And your son wouldn't have been there if he hadn't been caught shoplifting. Unfortunately, that's a crime."

"He's only eight," the mother said, getting shushed immediately by both her husband and the attorney.

"And where were you that he slipped away and went to the hardware store by himself?" Aimi asked.

"We'd rented a two-bedroom condo. He slipped out while I was on the phone," the mother said. "My husband was at the beach." She turned to the mediator. "He's never done this before."

"If I may ask one more question?" Aimi said.

Their attorney looked at them, then nodded, giving his approval.

"Why do you think irreparable harm has been done? Have you put him in counseling because of this incident?"

"No, but he said— " The mother clamped her lips shut.

"Said what?" the mediator asked.

The mother shook her head, agony showing on her face as she looked at the attorney, whose face was taut with frustration. He leaned in and whispered something to her, to which she nodded.

"Since the question has been asked and half-answered on the record, I'll finish it," the attorney said. "The boy said he had more fun with the sheriff than he'd ever had with his parents. They played a game, the sheriff showed him around the jail, and made him some hot chocolate."

Jackson grinned now. He'd liked that kid.

"So this lawsuit is because your child likes Jackson Smith better than you?" Aimi asked.

"We both work full time," the silent-till-now Dad said. "We try hard to engage him, but it seems a stranger is capable of doing that better than we are with our own child."

The mediator stepped in. "I think it's fair to say this is a frivolous lawsuit and that's what I will tell the courts. If you wish to pursue it, you'll have to apply for a court date. There's nothing more here that I can do."

The parents slumped in their chairs as their attorney leaned in to confer quietly with them. Nodding his head, he stood and left without a word to Aimi, Jackson, or the mediator.

Jackson leaned toward Aimi. "I want to talk to them for a minute."

"I don't think that's a bad thing, as long as James and I are here to witness it."

He looked at the parents, both downtrodden, worried, and clearly tired. "Your son is a great kid. I knew right away he'd never done something like this before."

"Really? He's told us that, but, well, we don't know what to believe."

"He's no juvenile delinquent. I purposely put a bit of fear into him so he'd realize the severity of what he'd done. I doubt he'll do it again. In my opinion, he just wants a little more time with you."

"That's hard to find these days," the father said.

"I know, but he's worth it."

They both nodded, giving Jackson the feeling that this family would be all right. With that, James departed, the parents right behind him, leaving only Jackson and Aimi in the room.

"Well, for my first case in my solo practice, you sure made it easy for me."

"And you helped my sister. I can't believe Julie's divorce is all agreed to and signed. She even got to keep Garvey. How did you manage all that?"

"A few well-timed suggestions for her attorney. It helped that the private detective Julie hired on your recommendation caught him living it up when he said he didn't have any money."

"I cannot thank you enough. She actually laughed when I spoke with her last week. Laughed!" Jackson said, pulling Aimi from her chair and onto his lap.

"Jackson! This is a meeting room in the courthouse."

"So?"

"I'm trying to garner a good reputation here."

"Oh, I can make quite certain you have a reputation with the courts."

She punched him lightly in the chest, then wound her arms around his neck. "You know what I mean."

"I do. It's just become very hard to keep my hands off you," he said, reminding her how good they were together with a kiss.

"I know the feeling," Aimi said. "I know it very well."

EPILOGUE

"I hear our sheriff is engaged?" the person on the other end of the phone said to Gladys.

"Yes, and they're all moved in together." She ran her hand along the leather arm of her easy chair.

"That worked out rather well."

"Very well. And have you made the donation to the fund for the women's shelter expansion?"

"Yes. That's a lot of money for what will probably stay a pretty small shelter."

"Big or small, it's the purpose it serves. Thank you for all you do for me."

"Anytime, Gladys, but one of these days I'll get you to the city so we can have a proper chat over dinner at a nice restaurant."

"And leave my beloved Willow Bay? I don't think so."

"I'll wear you down, you know."

"I have a pretty strong constitution."

"Don't I know it? Until next time."

Gladys hung up the phone and contemplated recent events. If she hadn't seen those men running from Aimi

Larson's office, would things have turned out as well? She shuddered at the possibilities.

Getting up from her desk, she went and poured herself an after-dinner sherry. Sometimes, it got lonely here. The town kept her company, but at times like this, when something she'd had a hand in, albeit a small one, had turned out so well, it would be nice to talk to someone about it. Maybe she'd take Henry up on his offer of dinner.

One of these days.

~~~

Thank you for reading **Chances Are**, the third story in the Willow Bay series. While this series can be read in any order, the next one in the series is **Tender Tide** (Ex-marine carpenter Luke and his neighbor, Jasmin, who helps her parents with horse rides on the beach.) If you enjoyed this book, please consider leaving a review wherever you prefer, and know that it would be greatly appreciated.

For new release information and news about Laurie Ryan, please join her **newsletter at www.laurieryanauthor.com.**
~~~

NOTE/ACKNOWLEDGEMENTS

When Aimi Larson came to Dana's rescue in Last Resort, the first Willow Bay story, I knew she needed her own book. And Jackson Smith was the perfect foil to her sassy, strong-willed personality. This was a fun story to write. And now, as I'm deep into writing the next story, Tender Tide, it's been nice to revisit this one during final edits.

I want to give my editor an extra special nod for her help with this story. Because of her expertise, the story became stronger, more believable, and more consistent. Any mistakes in processes are my own, not hers, but I'm very grateful for her eyes and knowledge.

I'm also more than excited with the covers for these stories and give a shout out to Richard Rodriguez, who gets my vision. And my critique partners: Lavada Dee and Faye Avalon. And to Marie Tuhart, who's been my sounding board and bearer of reason.

Thank you all! And to my readers, you have my heartfelt gratitude.

BOOKLIST

Contemporary romance stories by Laurie Ryan

Willow Bay Series
Last Resort
Finding Home
Chances Are
Tender Tide

Tropical Persuasions Series
Stolen Treasures
Pirate's Promise
Dare to Love

Standalone
Rudy's Heart
Lost and Found
Northern Lights
Healing Love
(also part of the Holiday Magic anthology)

Women's Fiction by Laurie Ryan
Show Me

Fantasy by Laurie Ryan
Survival
Enlightenment
Birthright
Awakening
Wolf's Call

AUTHOR BIO

Laurie Ryan writes fantasy and contemporary romance. Growing up a devoted reader, Laurie Ryan immersed herself in the diverse works of authors like Tolkien and Woodiwiss. She is passionate about every aspect of a book: beginning, middle, and end. She can't arrive to a movie five minutes late, has never been able to read the end of a book before the beginning, and is a strong believer in reading the book before seeing the movie.

Laurie lives in the beautiful Pacific Northwest, in the shadow of Mt. Rainier and a short drive to beach-walking next to the Pacific Ocean, with her handsome, he-can-fix-anything husband.

You can find more about Laurie Ryan at:

www.laurieryanauthor.com

A Sneak Peek at the Third Book in the Willow Bay Series

Tender Tide
by Laurie Ryan

CHAPTER ONE

Gladys Hawthorne sat in her comfortable recliner staring out the window at the September sunshine, so rare on the coast this time of year. After last winter's abundance of rain, no one in Willow Bay looked forward to winter. Summer had been a glorious respite from mud puddles and flooded roads. She, for one, did not look forward to traipsing around in the rain. Her old bones complained more these days than ever before. Still, it was the only way to keep an eye on her town.

That's how she thought of Willow Bay, as hers. She'd moved here after her husband's death several years ago and had adopted the town, as the town had adopted her. Except the town had no idea who Gladys Hawthorne really was. To them, she was the local street person, always around, eyes wide open, and always with an opinion of how the town should be run. She'd harangued Josh Morgan, Willow Bay's Mayor, more times than she could count, yet he continued to treat her like a friend and always asked after her welfare. Did she have enough food? Did she want a place to sleep?

That wife of his, Dana, had really helped him to relax. Gladys smiled, knowing she'd had a part in making that happen. Same with Bernie, who owned the Square Peg pizza parlor, and her husband, Paul. A few choice words in the right ears had gotten them together and now they were expecting a baby, just like Dana and Josh.

Dana's friend Aimi and Willow Bay's sheriff… That had been the dangerous one. A deluded stalker had come after Aimi and Jackson had been the only one who could keep her safe. And now they were planning their wedding. Gladys hadn't been able to help much with that one, but she'd done what she could and love, once again, had won out.

A deep sense of satisfaction filled Gladys as she sipped her morning tea out of a dainty, floral cup. Mornings were her favorite time of the day. So much promise. New problems to solve, people to help past their stubborn nature. Speaking of which…

Noise, like a tool box closing, sounded behind her and Luke Taylor walked from the kitchen into her sitting room, carrying said box. Construction and handyman work had certainly done right by the ex-marine. The man's tall frame had muscles in all the right places, honed for work, not for show. But show they did. She might be old, but she had eyes and could appreciate a handsome man. With that short, thick blond hair and those blue, blue eyes, Lucas Taylor was the quintessential boy next door.

Gladys tapped her lips with her finger as if shooshing a child. Luke was also very much a loner, something Gladys had mused about for some time now. With all he did to help others, he should be surrounded by the love of a good partner. And she'd finally come up with a solution for that.

"Leak's all fixed, Gladys."

"Thank you. You're a good man to come spur of the moment." She stood up and patted his arm. "And for keeping my secret."

"When are you going to let Willow Bay in on this whole 'not really a street person' thing?"

"When I'm good and ready, Luke Taylor. And not a moment before."

He shook his head. "You are an enigma, Miss Gladys. Not sure I'll ever understand you."

"Just keep fixing what breaks around here and we'll get along just fine." She pulled a check out of her housecoat pocket and handed it to him.

"I don't like taking your money."

"If you don't start taking more of it, you'll end up like my alter ego for real. You don't charge enough for what you do."

He shrugged, so Gladys dropped the subject and moved on to something much dearer to her heart. "So, how are your neighbors doing?"

"The Powters? As well as can be expected."

"That stroke of Katherine's was a close call, wasn't it?"

"Too close. They almost didn't get her to the hospital in time." The frown on Luke's face showed his concern. "And Ned's health isn't great, either."

"I heard that their daughter has moved back home to help out."

Luke's eyes brightened for a moment and Gladys worked hard to keep her glee under wraps.

"Yep," he said.

"Jasmin was always such a lovely girl. I don't understand why she moved all the way to New York City." Gladys had lived there for years and it didn't hold a candle to the quiet, small town life of Willow Bay.

Luke shrugged, the scowl firmly back on his face. "Some people need change."

"Yes, they do, don't they? Sometimes, a chance like that helps you figure out where home really is."

Luke's sharp eyes watched Gladys with too much intelligence. She'd planted the seed. Now all she could do was pray that it would grow. Maybe with the occasional nudge, but too much interference would send both these introverts in opposite directions.

That couldn't happen. They were perfect for each other. So Gladys changed the subject to safer ground. "You going to the Cannery Park opening?"

"Yep. Want a ride?"

"Oh, no, dearie." She put a hand on his arm again and walked him to the back door. "Wouldn't do to have me seen on the arm of a hunk like you. Everybody would start thinking I'm off the market."

Luke's frown disappeared as he chuckled. "Like I said, you're an enigma." He reached down to kiss her cheek, then left with a wave. Because of her need for subterfuge, he would take the alley to the side street and walk around to his truck.

"Such a good boy," she said, closing the door and headed for her bedroom. It was time to get dressed and out and about to see what was happening in her town today.

~~~

For more information about Tender Tide, visit Laurie Ryan's website at www.laurieryanauthor.com.
~~~